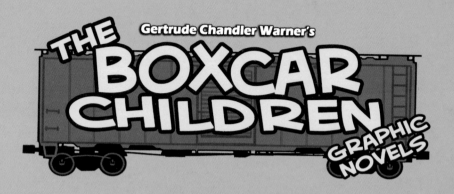

Gertrude Chandler Warner's

THE BOXCAR CHILDREN GRAPHIC NOVELS

BICYCLE MYSTERY

The Aldens are making the journey to their Aunt Jane's house for an overnight bicycle trip. On their first night, though, the children are caught in a rainstorm. They have to take shelter in an old, abandoned house. There, a most unusual mystery—a lost dog— finds them! Can the Boxcar Children figure out where the dog belongs?

THE BOXCAR CHILDREN
GRAPHIC NOVELS

THE BOXCAR CHILDREN
SURPRISE ISLAND
THE YELLOW HOUSE MYSTERY
MYSTERY RANCH
MIKE'S MYSTERY
BLUE BAY MYSTERY
SNOWBOUND MYSTERY
TREE HOUSE MYSTERY
THE HAUNTED CABIN MYSTERY
THE AMUSEMENT PARK MYSTERY
THE PIZZA MYSTERY
THE CASTLE MYSTERY
THE WOODSHED MYSTERY
THE LIGHTHOUSE MYSTERY
MOUNTAIN TOP MYSTERY
HOUSEBOAT MYSTERY
BICYCLE MYSTERY
MYSTERY IN THE SAND

Gertrude Chandler Warner's

THE BOXCAR CHILDREN
BICYCLE MYSTERY

Adapted by Joeming Dunn
Illustrated by Ben Dunn

Henry Alden

Jessie Alden

Watch

Violet Alden

Benny Alden

Visit us at www.albertwhitman.com.

Copyright © 2010 by Abdo Consulting Group, Inc. All rights reserved. Published in 2011 by Albert Whitman & Company by arrangement with Abdo Consulting Group, Inc. No part of this book may be reproduced in any form without written permission from the publisher. THE BOXCAR CHILDREN® is a registered trademark of Albert Whitman & Company.

Adapted by Joeming Dunn
Illustrated by Ben Dunn
Colored by Robby Bevard
Lettered by Doug Dlin
Edited by Stephanie Hedlund
Interior layout and design by Kristen Fitzner Denton
Cover art by Ben Dunn
Book design and packaging by Shannon Eric Denton

Library of Congress Cataloging-in-Publication Data
is available from the Library of Congress.

10 9 8 7 6 5 4 3 2 1 LB 15 14 13 12 11

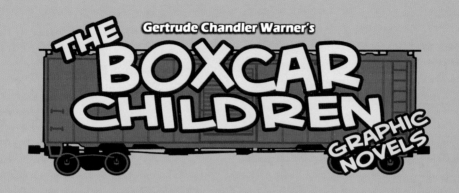

BICYCLE MYSTERY

Contents

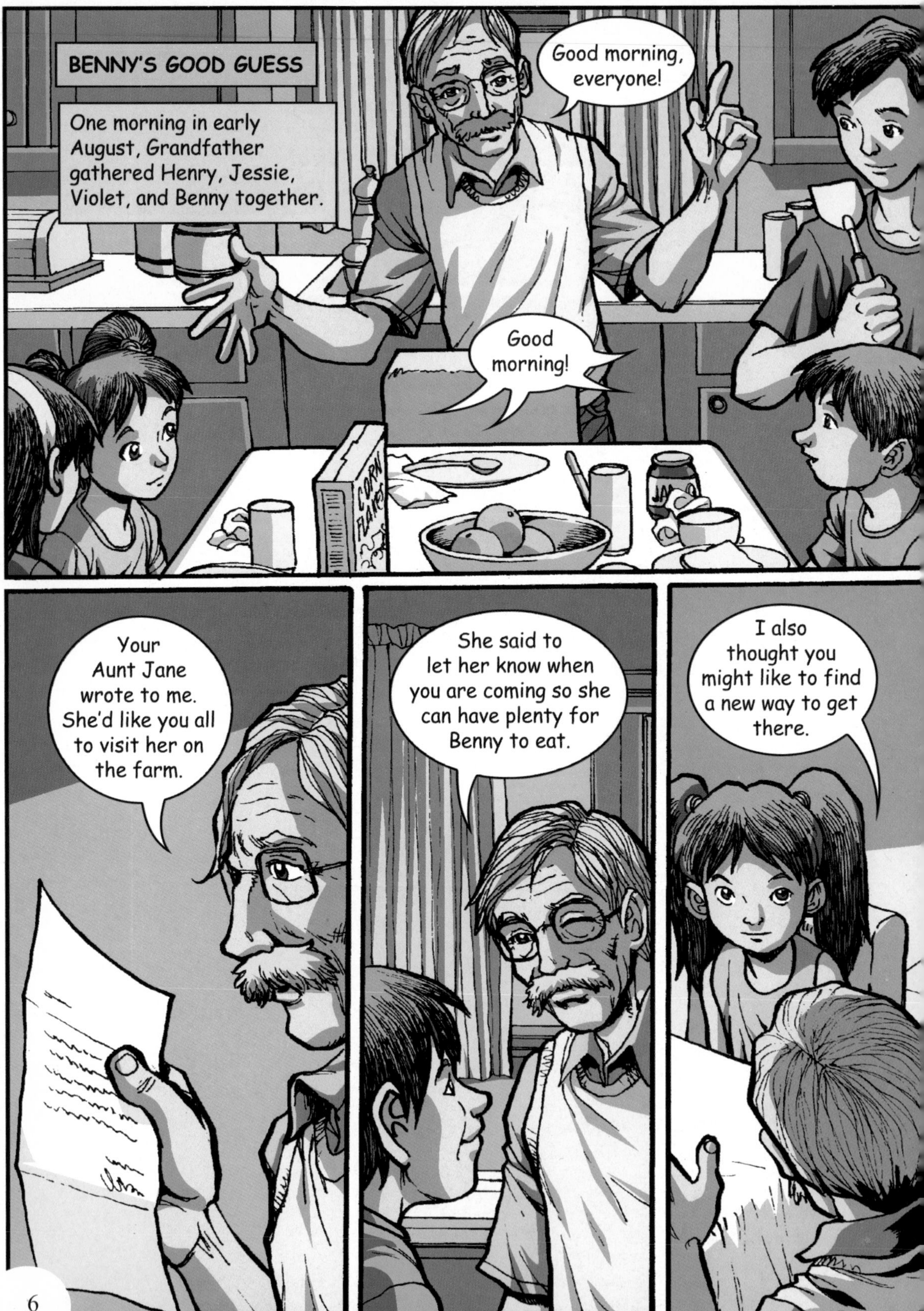
BENNY'S GOOD GUESS
One morning in early August, Grandfather gathered Henry, Jessie, Violet, and Benny together.
Good morning, everyone!
Good morning!
CORN FLAKES
Your Aunt Jane wrote to me. She'd like you all to visit her on the farm.
She said to let her know when you are coming so she can have plenty for Benny to eat.
I also thought you might like to find a new way to get there.

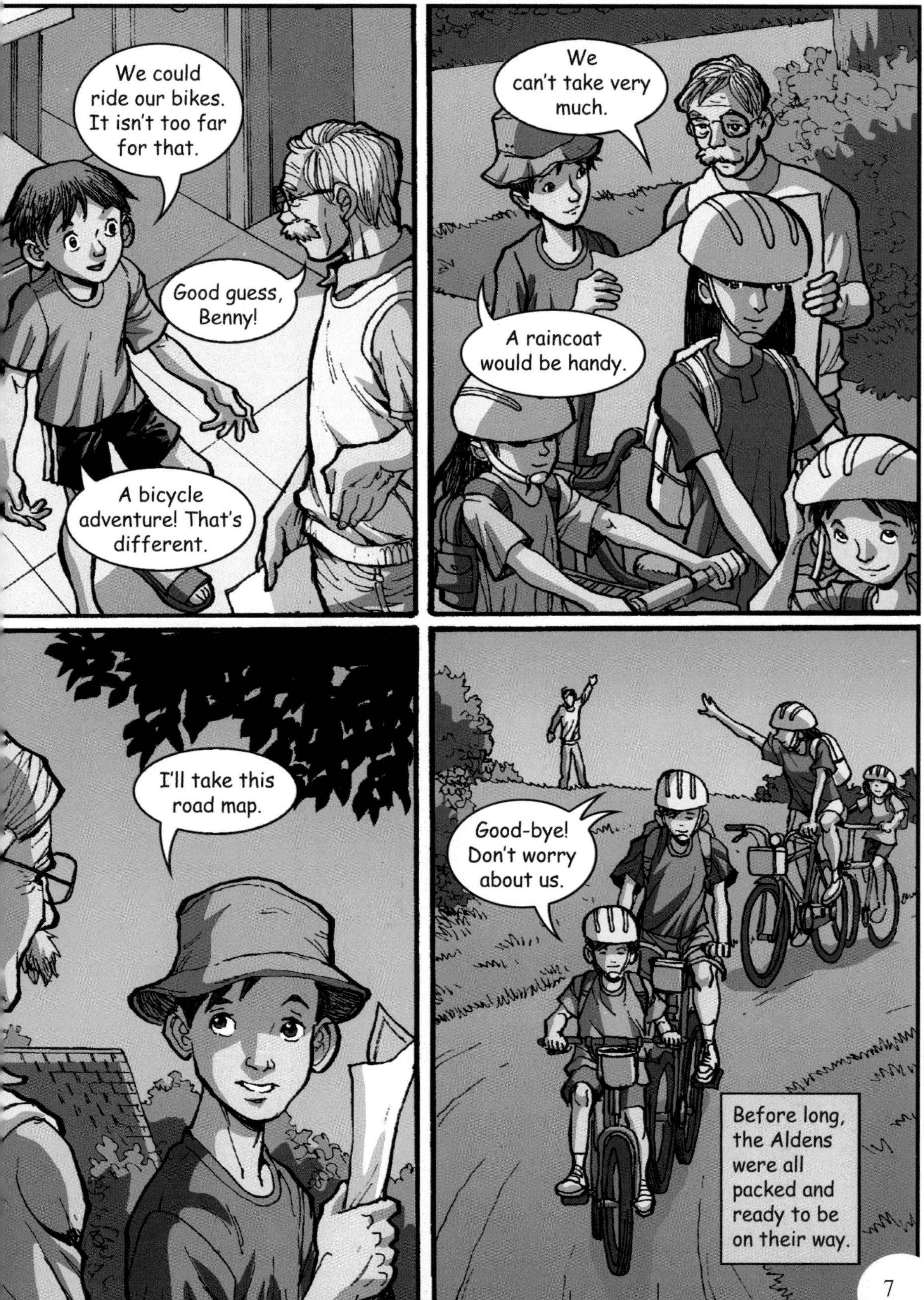
We could ride our bikes. It isn't too far for that.
Good guess, Benny!
A bicycle adventure! That's different.
We can't take very much.
A raincoat would be handy.
I'll take this road map.
Good-bye! Don't worry about us.
Before long, the Aldens were all packed and ready to be on their way.

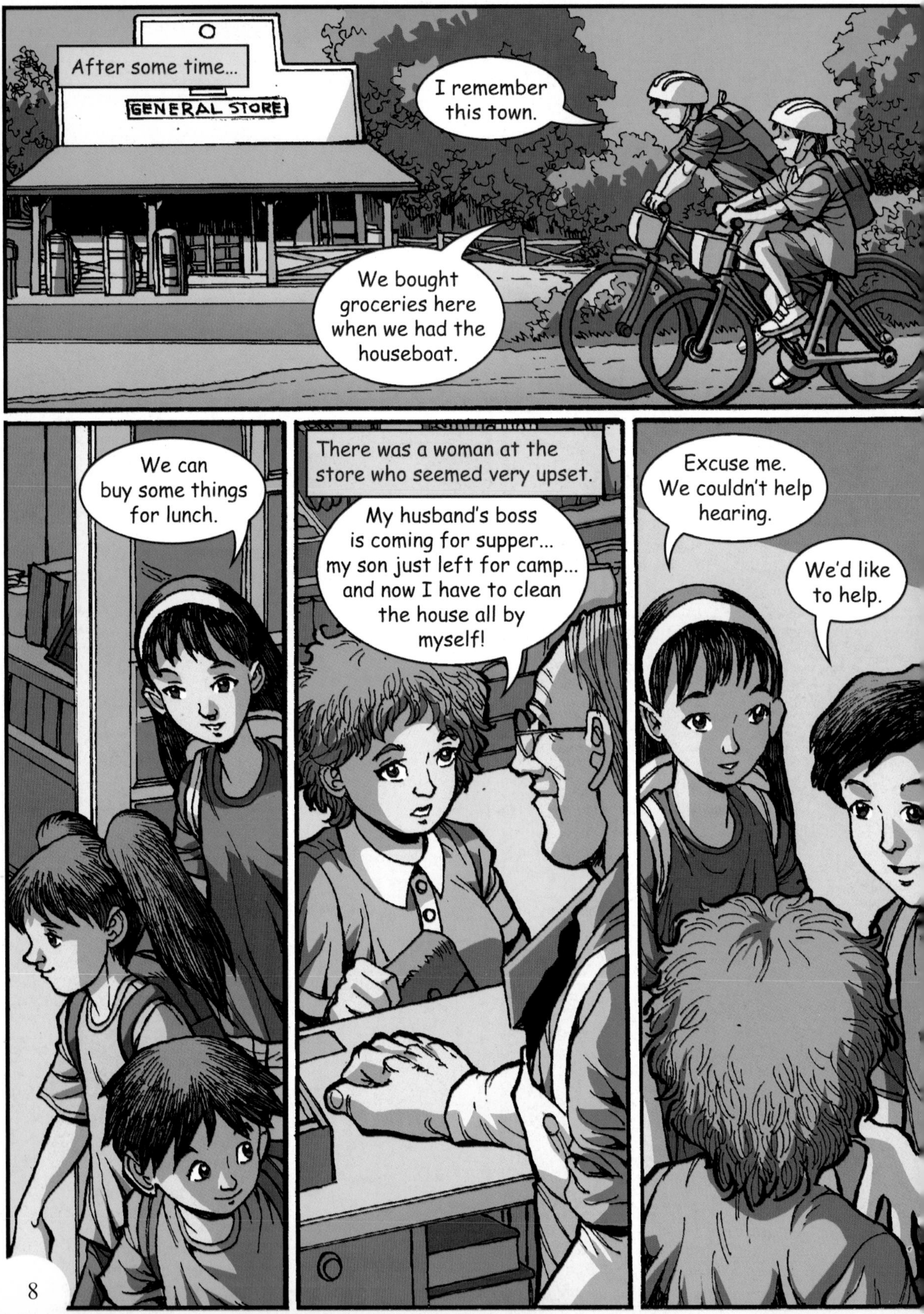
After some time...
GENERAL STORE
I remember this town.
We bought groceries here when we had the houseboat.
We can buy some things for lunch.
There was a woman at the store who seemed very upset.
My husband's boss is coming for supper... my son just left for camp... and now I have to clean the house all by myself!
Excuse me. We couldn't help hearing.
We'd like to help.

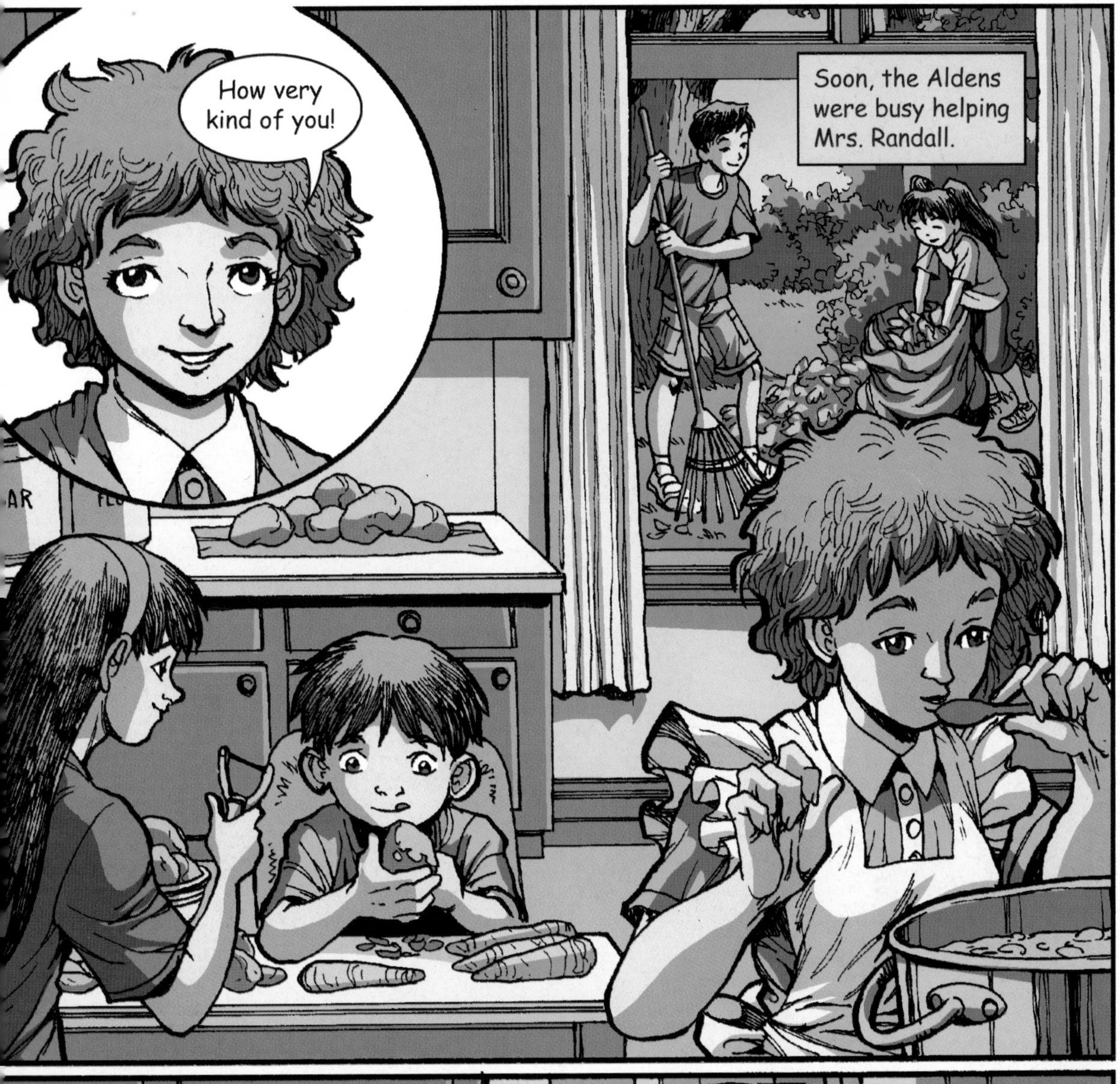
How very kind of you!
Soon, the Aldens were busy helping Mrs. Randall.

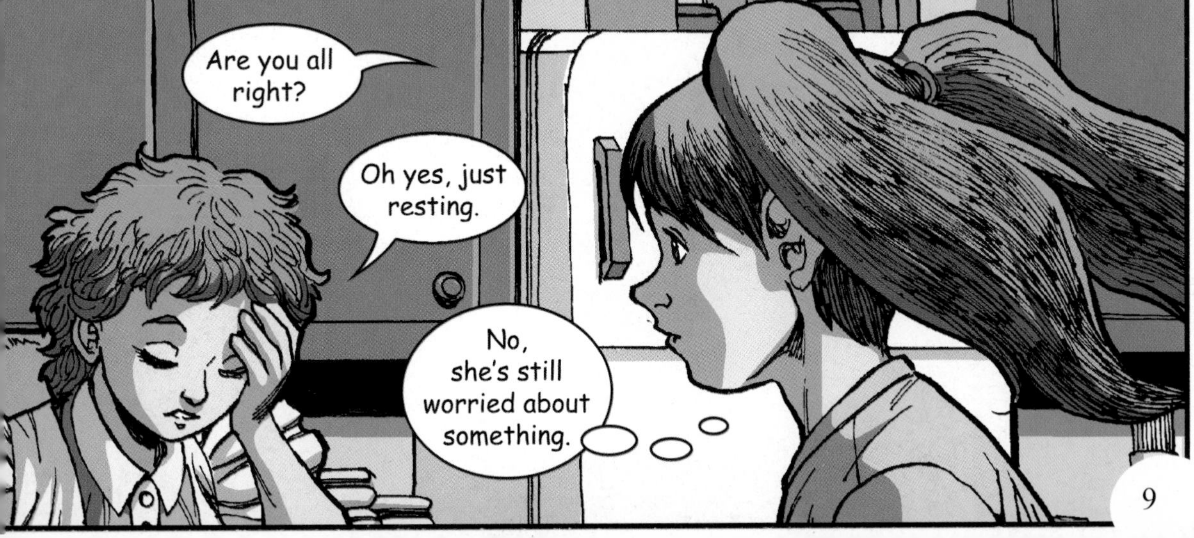
Are you all right?
Oh yes, just resting.
No, she's still worried about something.

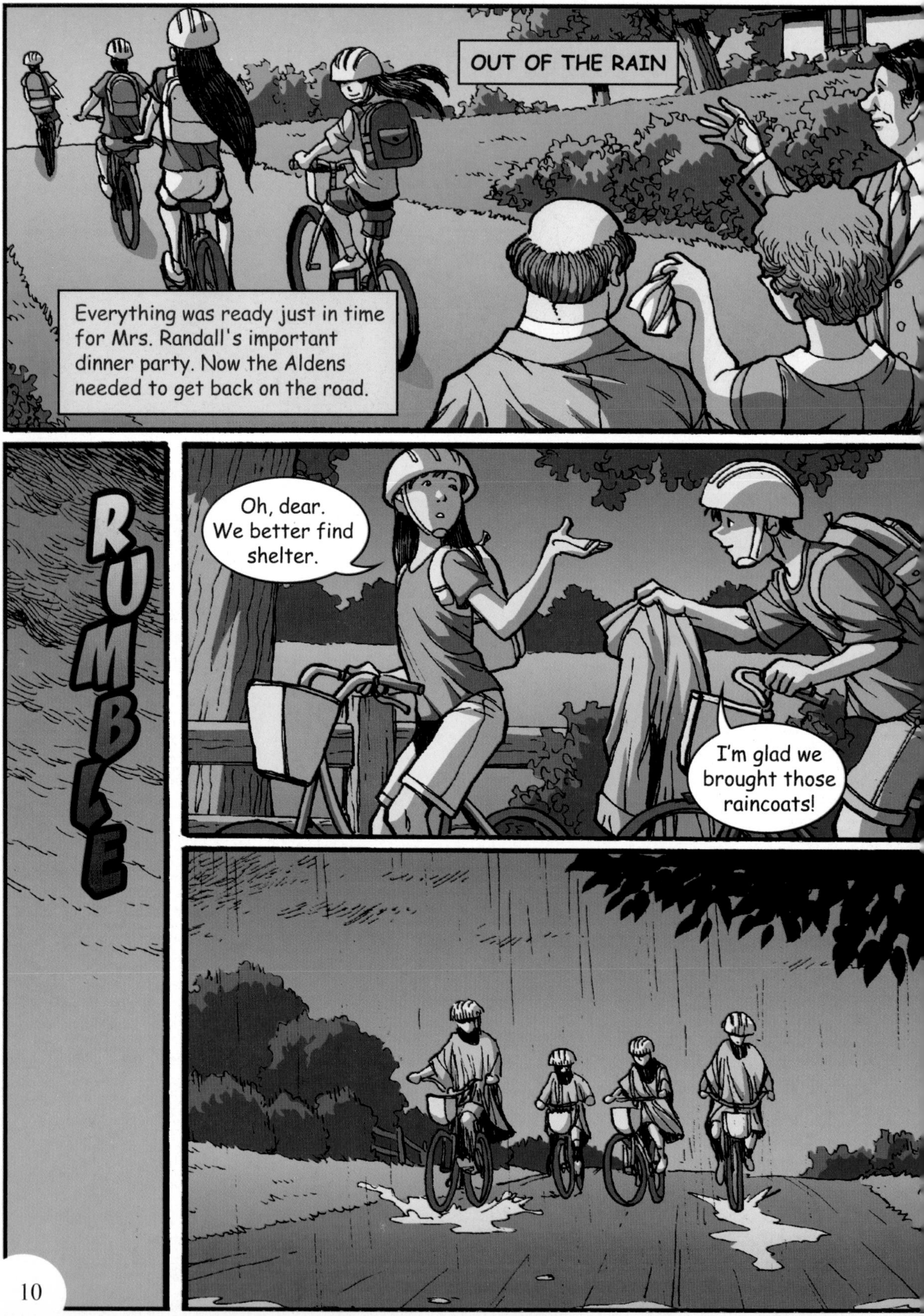
OUT OF THE RAIN
Everything was ready just in time for Mrs. Randall's important dinner party. Now the Aldens needed to get back on the road.
RUMBLE
Oh, dear. We better find shelter.
I'm glad we brought those raincoats!

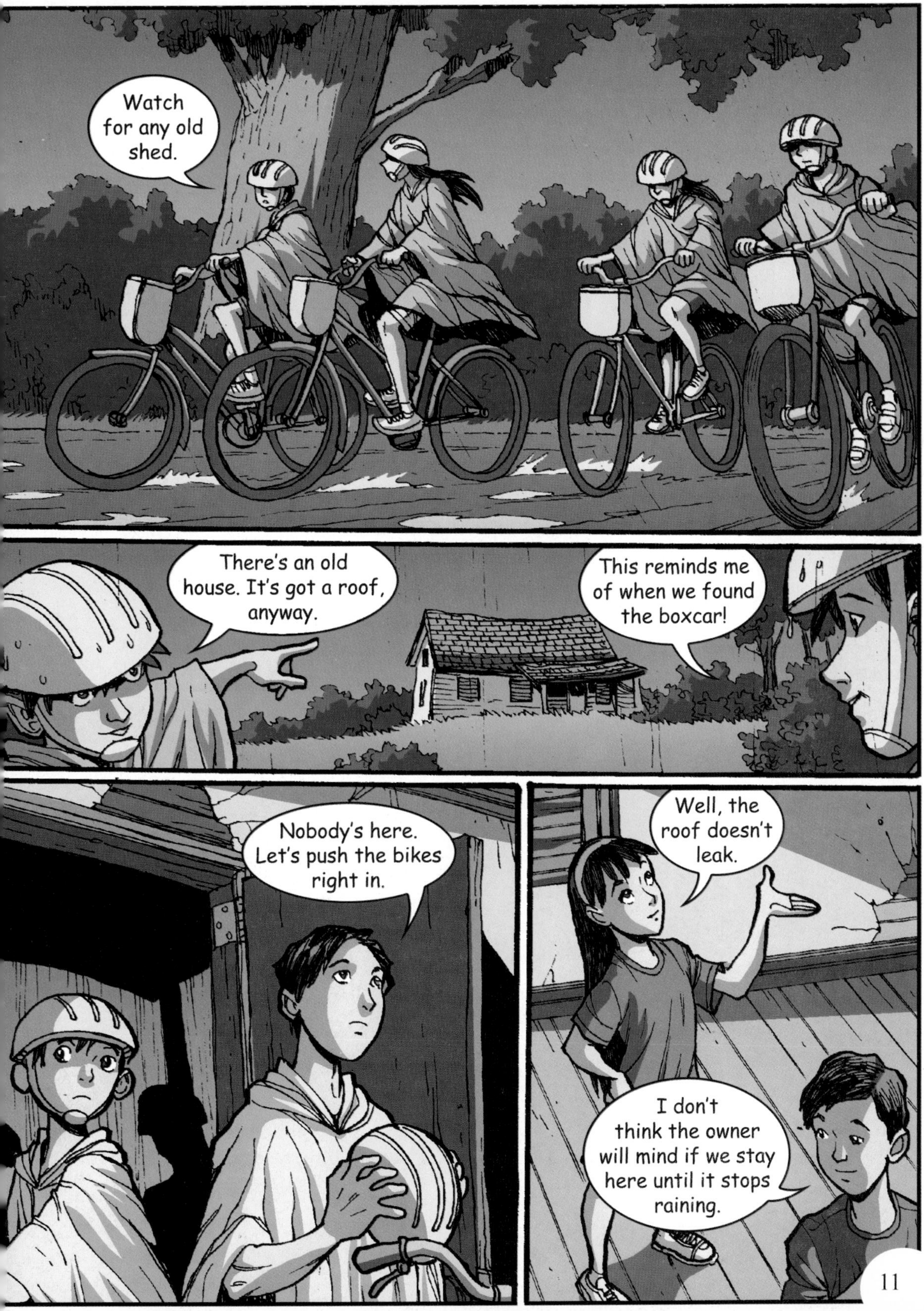
Watch for any old shed.
There's an old house. It's got a roof, anyway.
This reminds me of when we found the boxcar!
Nobody's here. Let's push the bikes right in.
Well, the roof doesn't leak.
I don't think the owner will mind if we stay here until it stops raining.

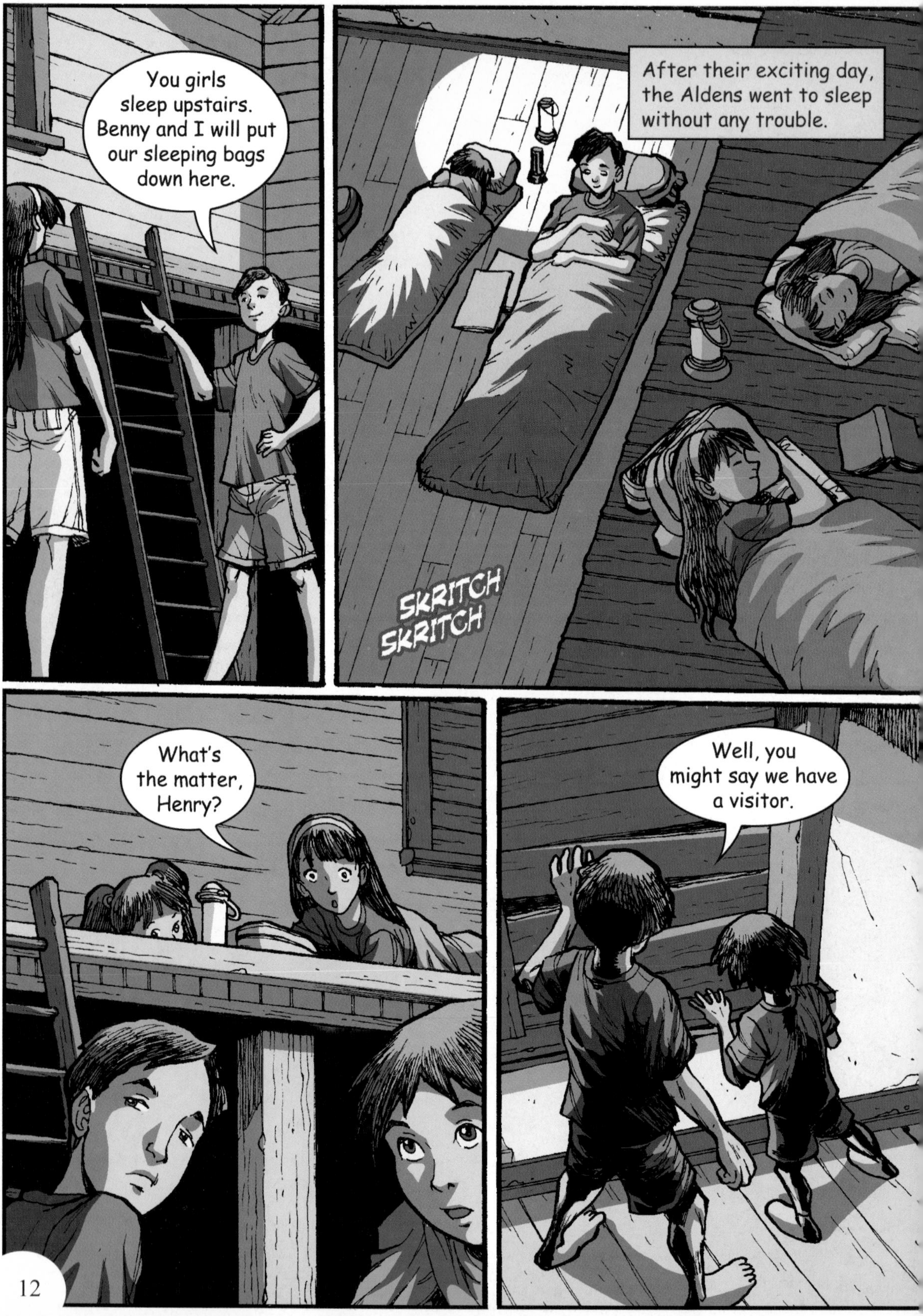
You girls sleep upstairs. Benny and I will put our sleeping bags down here.
After their exciting day, the Aldens went to sleep without any trouble.
SKRITCH SKRITCH
What's the matter, Henry?
Well, you might say we have a visitor.

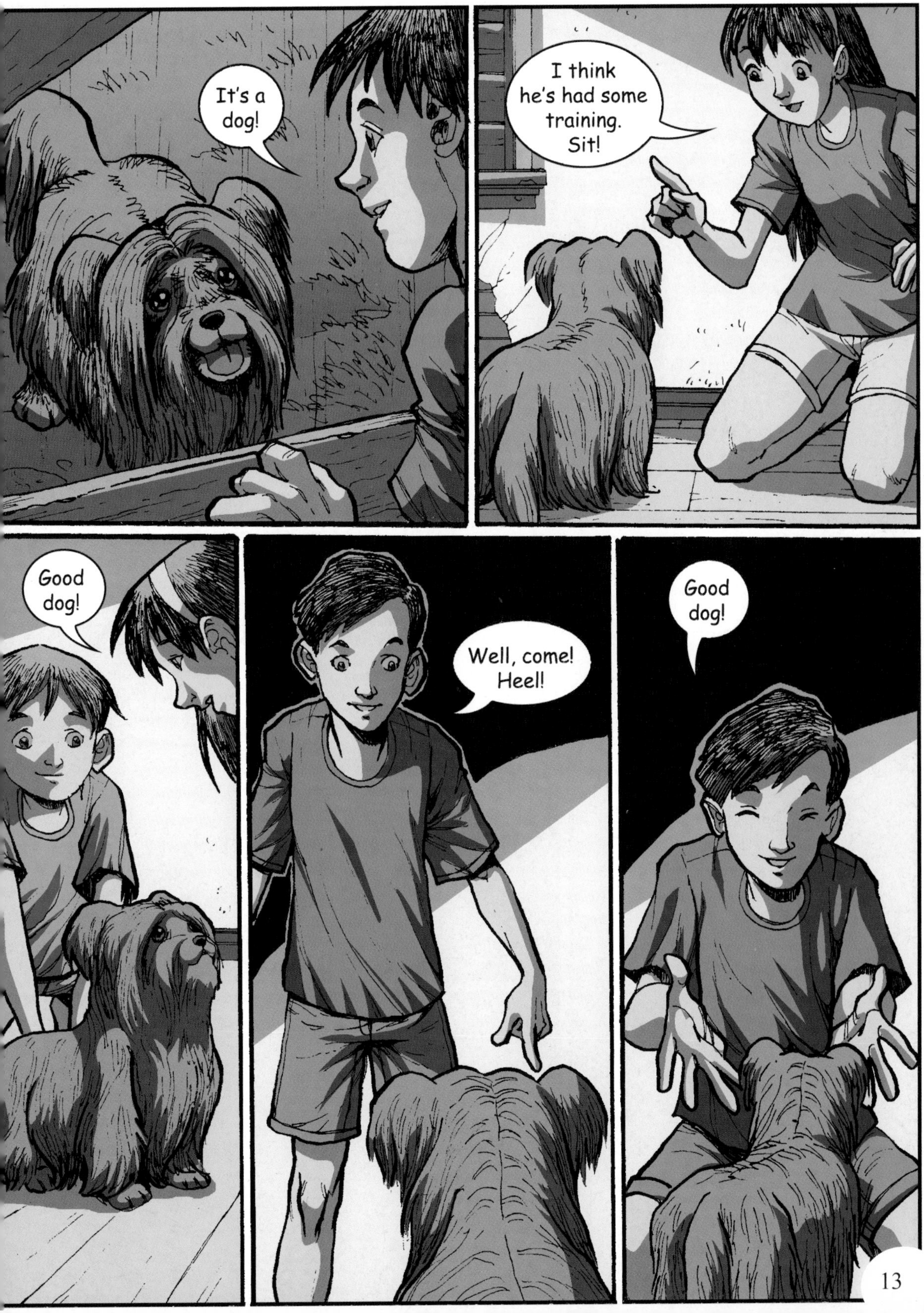
It's a dog!
I think he's had some training. Sit!
Good dog!
Well, come! Heel!
Good dog!

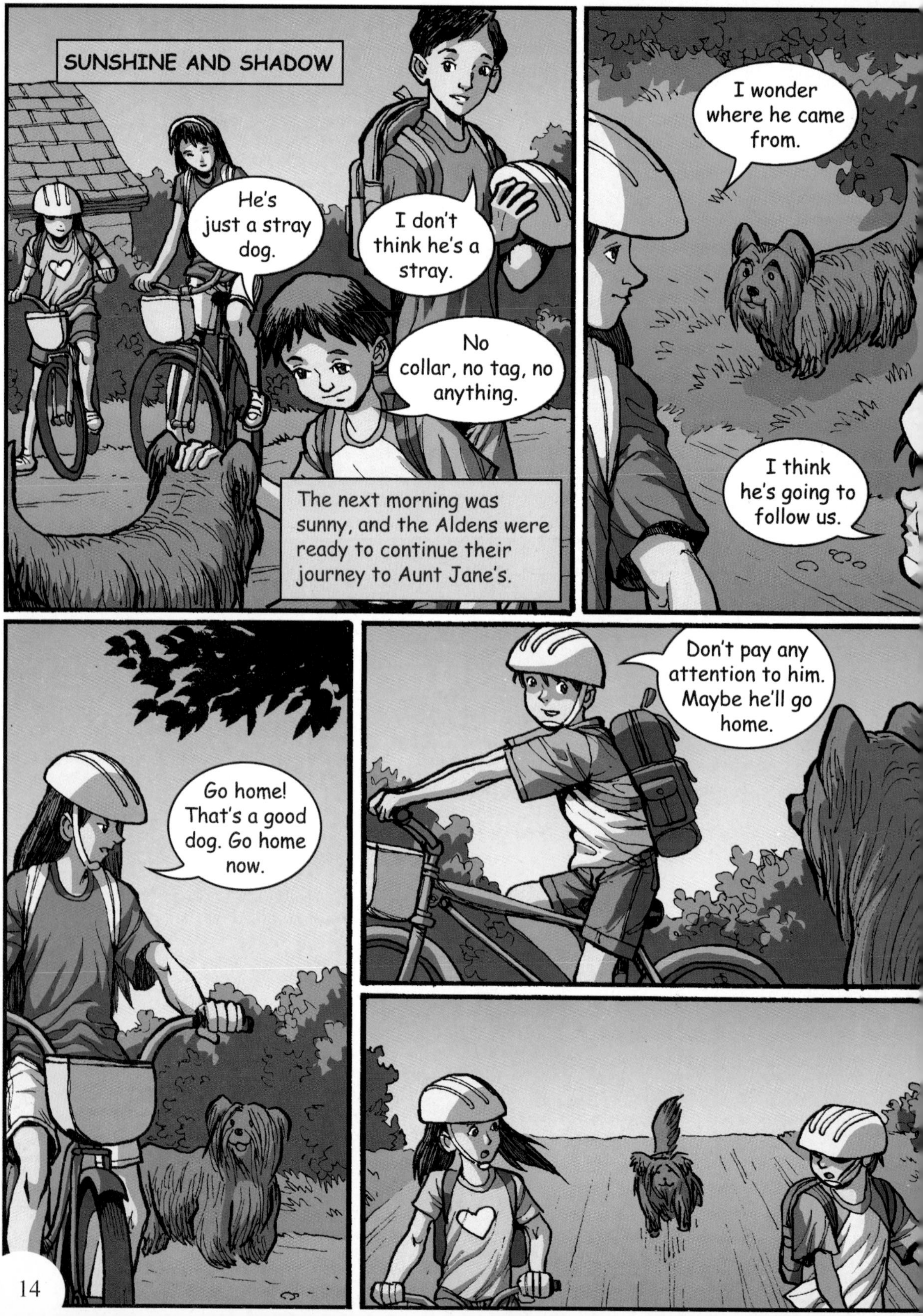
SUNSHINE AND SHADOW
The next morning was sunny, and the Aldens were ready to continue their journey to Aunt Jane's.
He's just a stray dog.
I don't think he's a stray.
No collar, no tag, no anything.
I wonder where he came from.
I think he's going to follow us.
Go home! That's a good dog. Go home now.
Don't pay any attention to him. Maybe he'll go home.

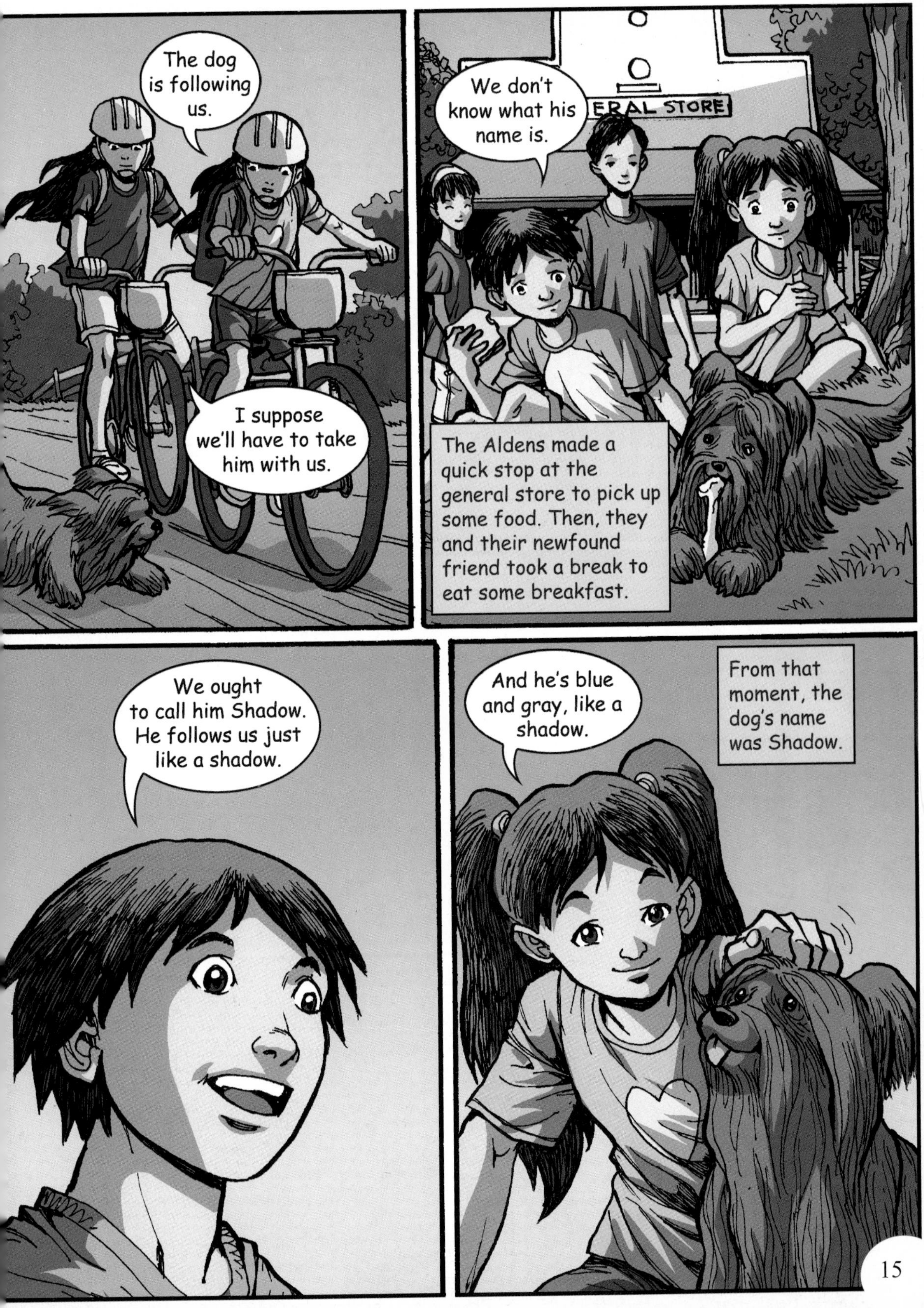
The dog is following us.
I suppose we'll have to take him with us.
ERAL STORE
We don't know what his name is.
The Aldens made a quick stop at the general store to pick up some food. Then, they and their newfound friend took a break to eat some breakfast.
We ought to call him Shadow. He follows us just like a shadow.
And he's blue and gray, like a shadow.
From that moment, the dog's name was Shadow.

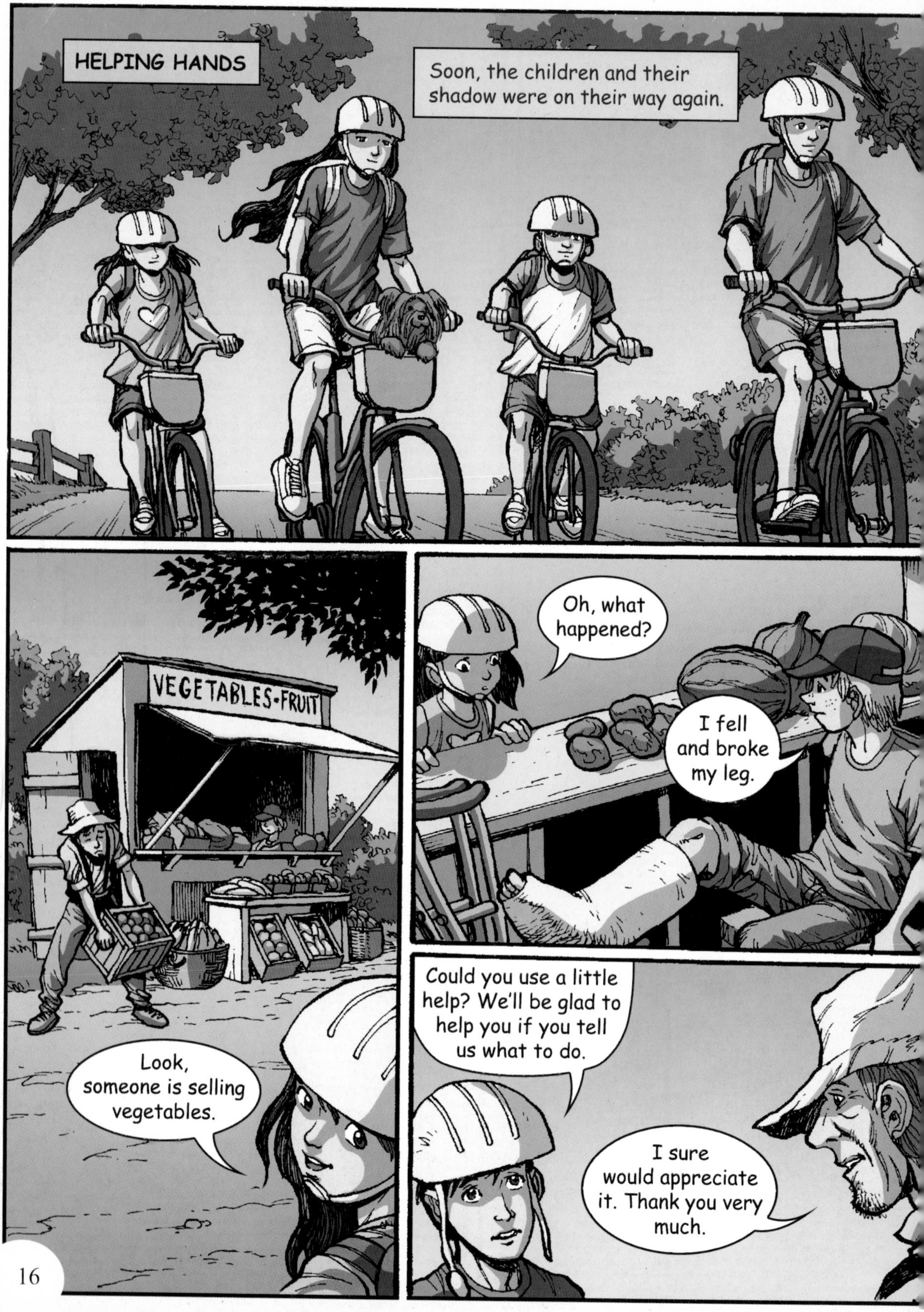
HELPING HANDS
Soon, the children and their shadow were on their way again.
VEGETABLES-FRUIT
Look, someone is selling vegetables.
Oh, what happened?
I fell and broke my leg.
Could you use a little help? We'll be glad to help you if you tell us what to do.
I sure would appreciate it. Thank you very much.

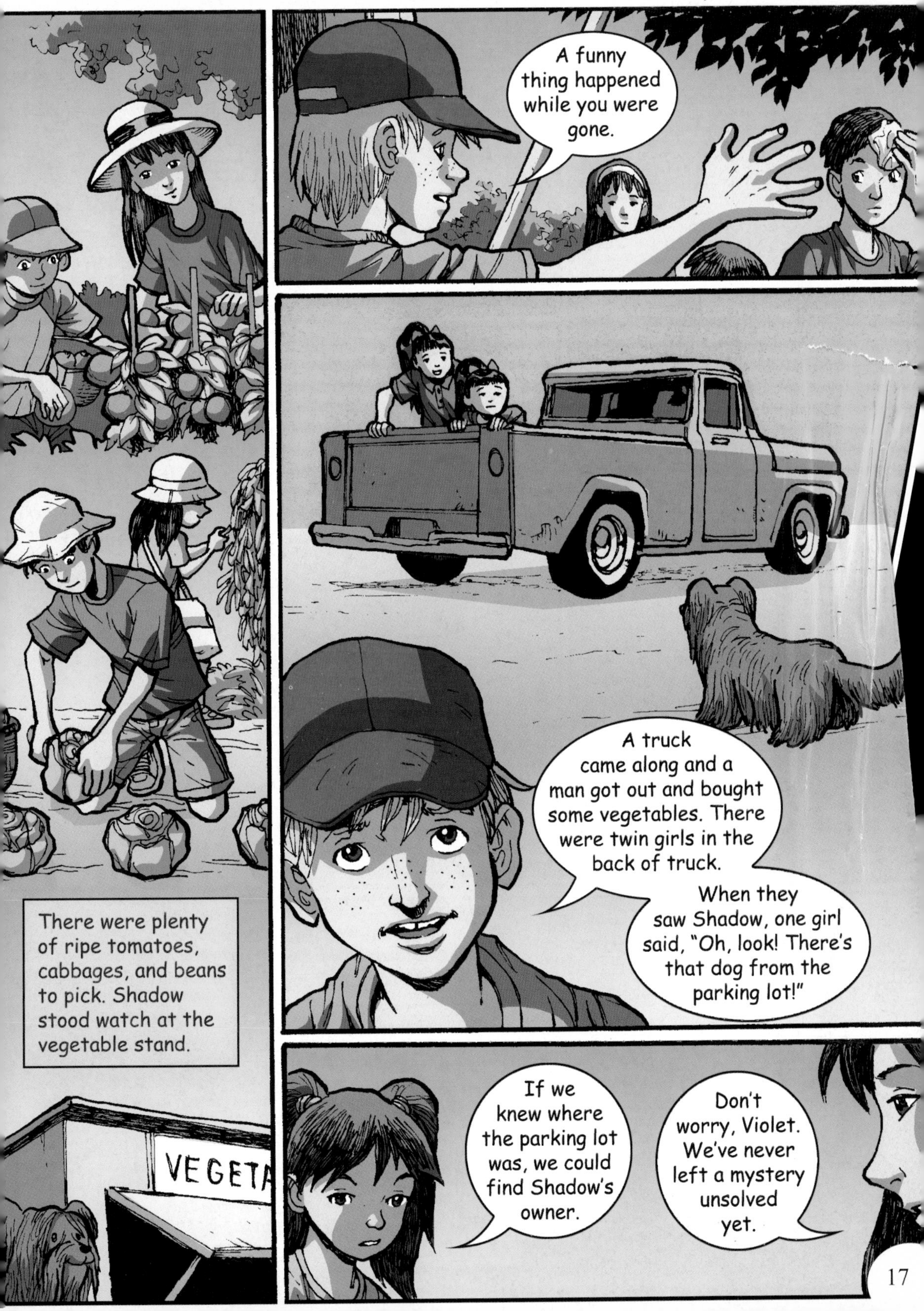

A funny thing happened while you were gone.
There were plenty of ripe tomatoes, cabbages, and beans to pick. Shadow stood watch at the vegetable stand.
A truck came along and a man got out and bought some vegetables. There were twin girls in the back of truck.
When they saw Shadow, one girl said, "Oh, look! There's that dog from the parking lot!"
VEGETA
If we knew where the parking lot was, we could find Shadow's owner.
Don't worry, Violet. We've never left a mystery unsolved yet.

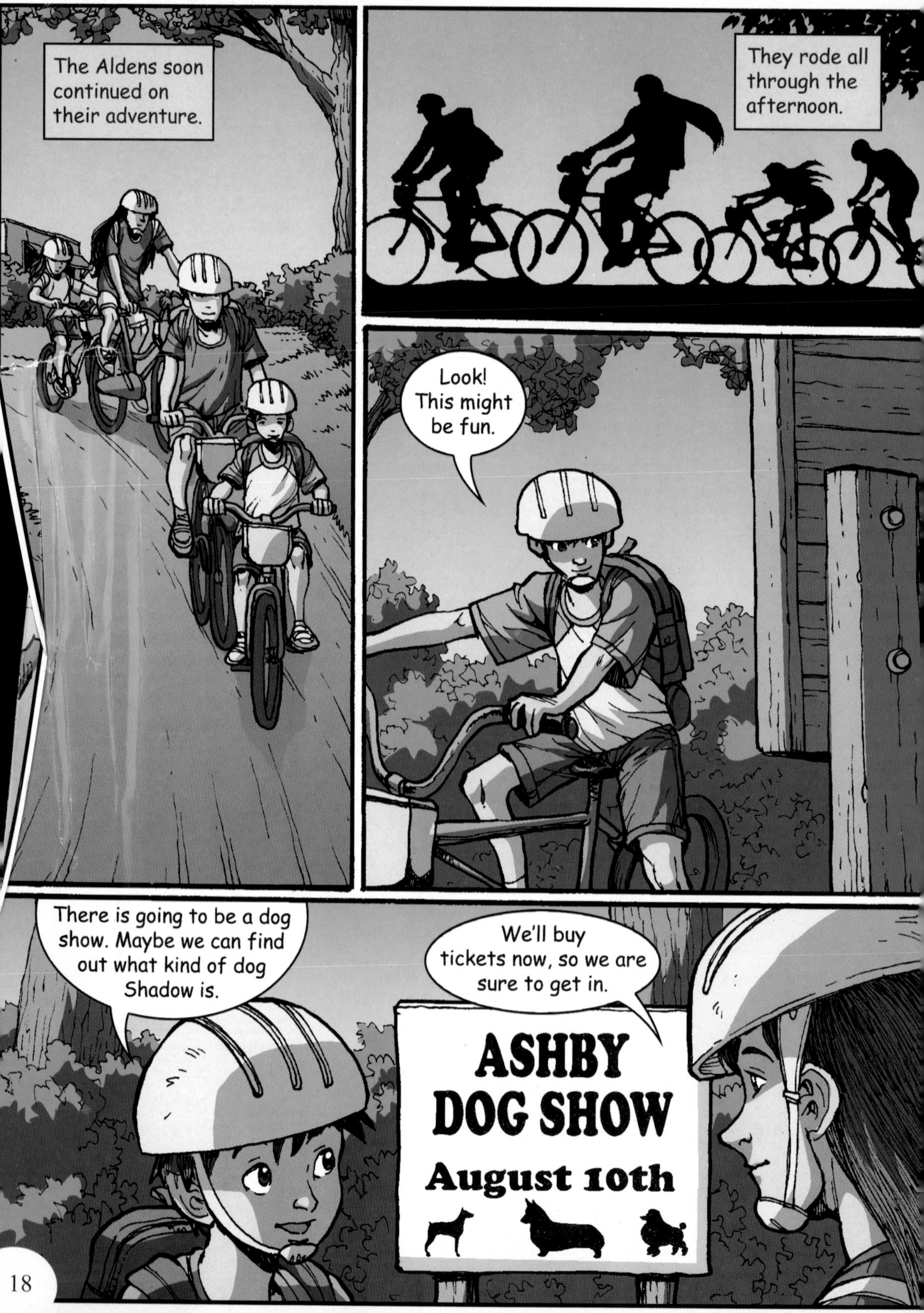

The Aldens soon continued on their adventure.
They rode all through the afternoon.
Look! This might be fun.
There is going to be a dog show. Maybe we can find out what kind of dog Shadow is.
We'll buy tickets now, so we are sure to get in.
ASHBY DOG SHOW
August 10th

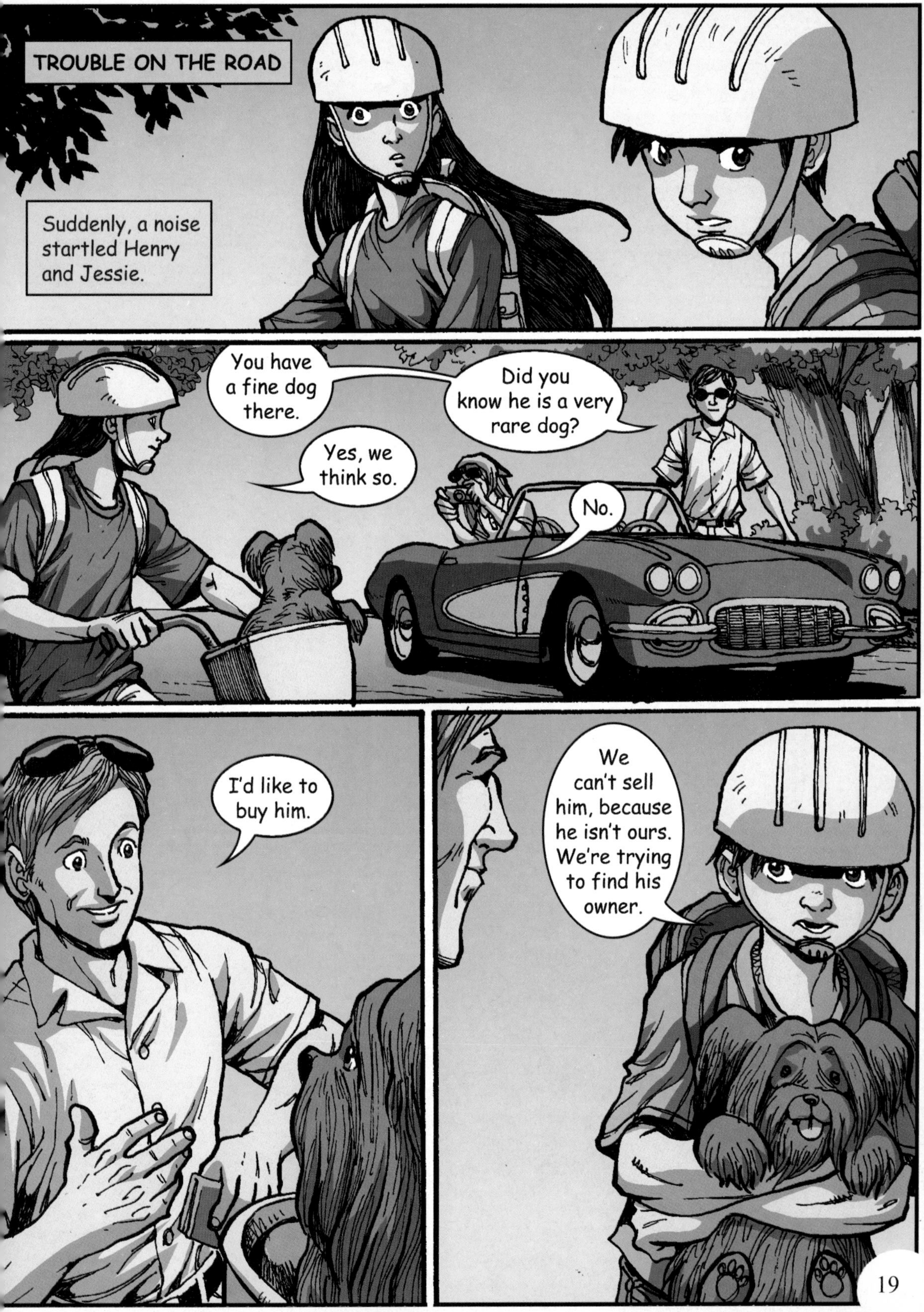
TROUBLE ON THE ROAD
Suddenly, a noise startled Henry and Jessie.
You have a fine dog there.
Did you know he is a very rare dog?
Yes, we think so.
No.
I'd like to buy him.
We can't sell him, because he isn't ours. We're trying to find his owner.

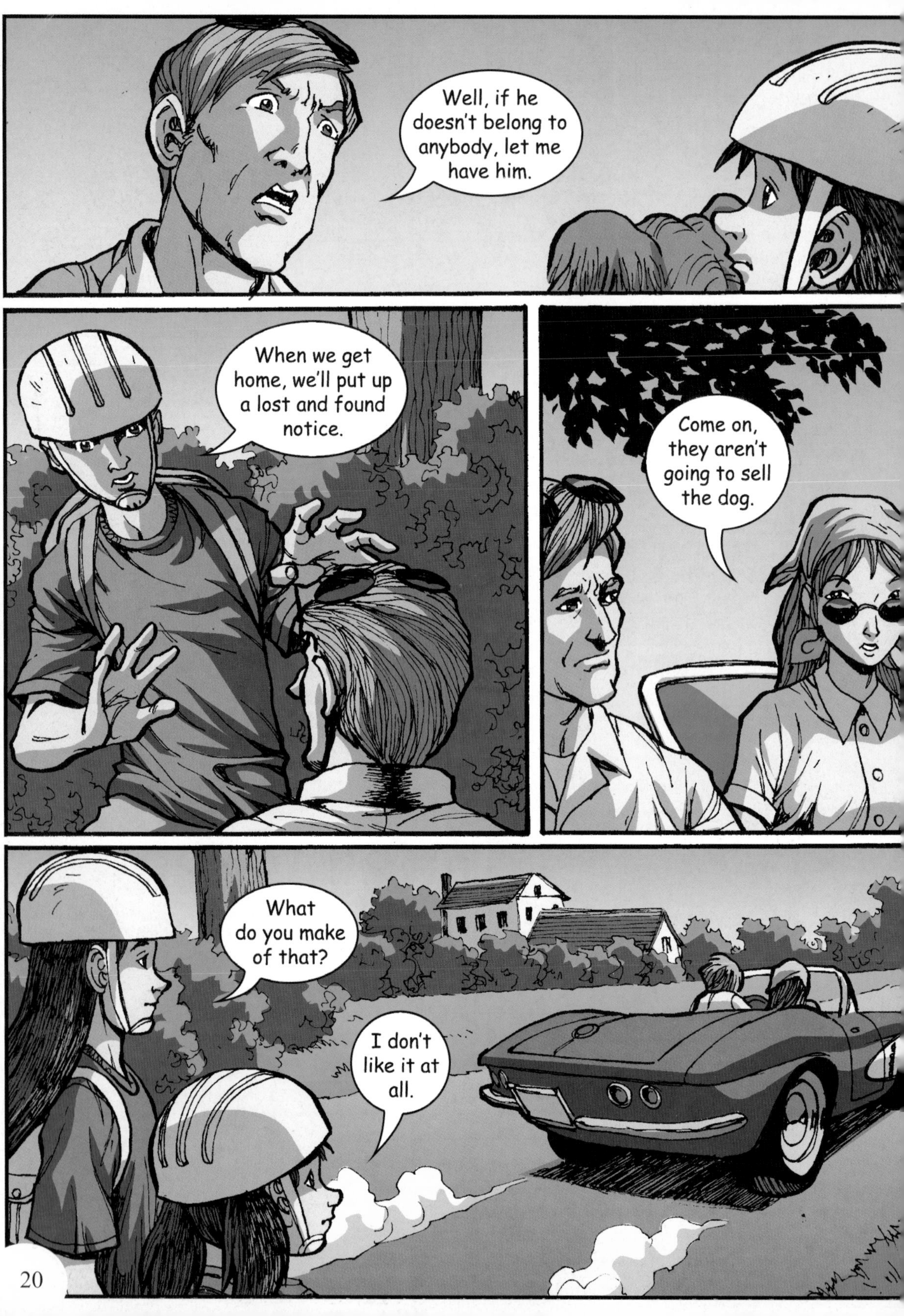
Well, if he doesn't belong to anybody, let me have him.
When we get home, we'll put up a lost and found notice.
Come on, they aren't going to sell the dog.
What do you make of that?
I don't like it at all.

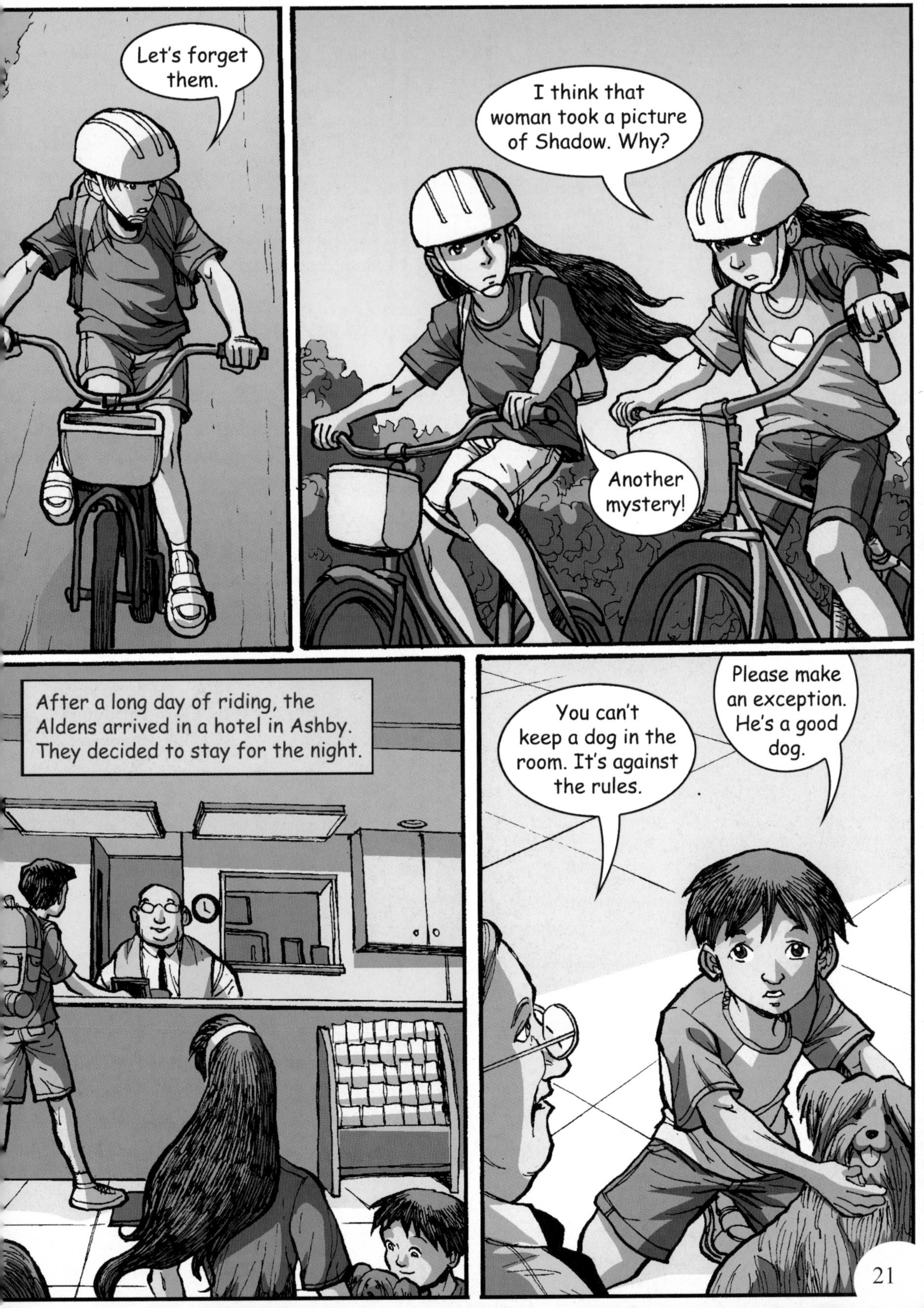

Let's forget them.
I think that woman took a picture of Shadow. Why?
Another mystery!
After a long day of riding, the Aldens arrived in a hotel in Ashby. They decided to stay for the night.
You can't keep a dog in the room. It's against the rules.
Please make an exception. He's a good dog.

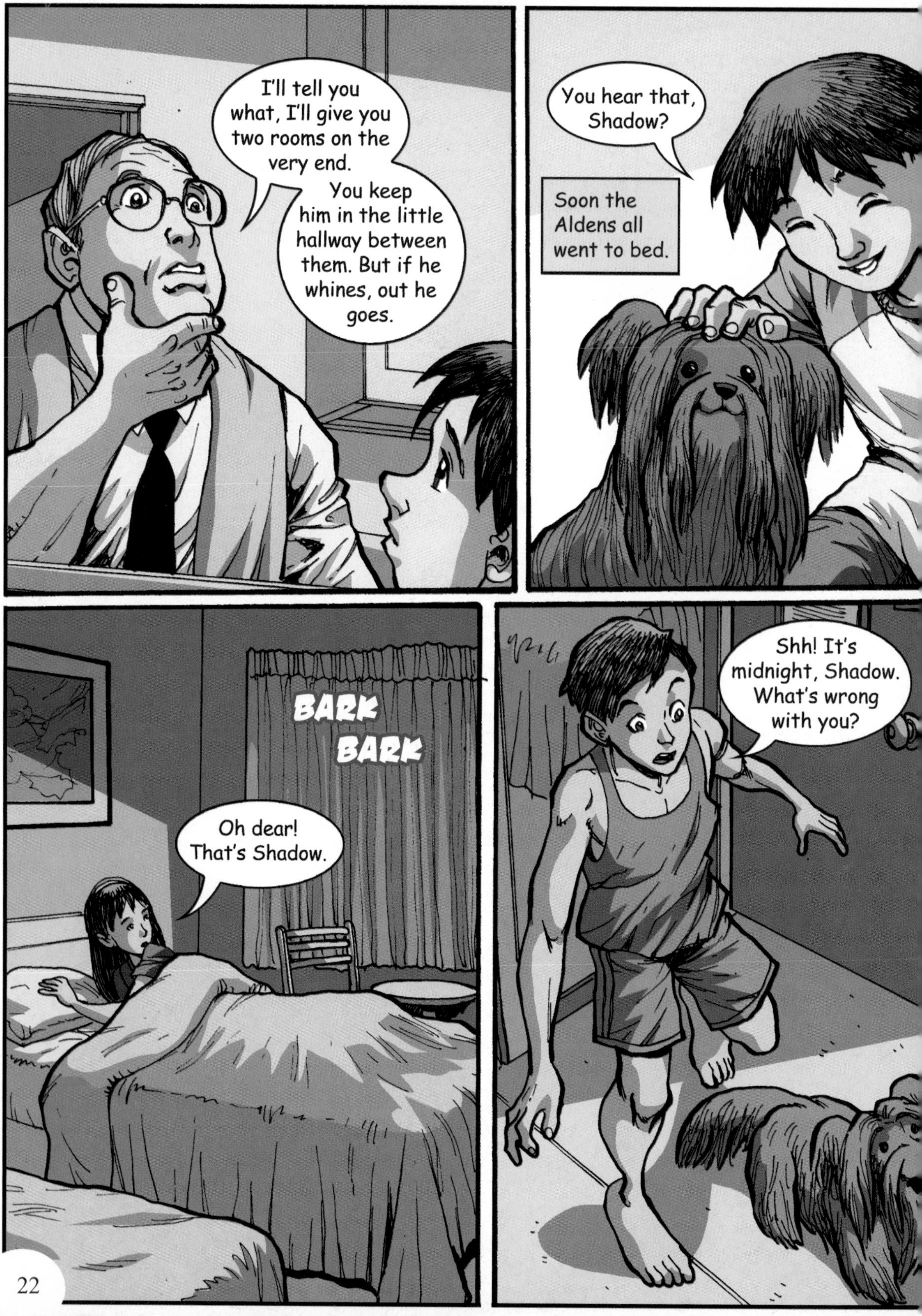
I'll tell you what, I'll give you two rooms on the very end.
You keep him in the little hallway between them. But if he whines, out he goes.
You hear that, Shadow?
Soon the Aldens all went to bed.
BARK
BARK
Oh dear! That's Shadow.
Shh! It's midnight, Shadow. What's wrong with you?

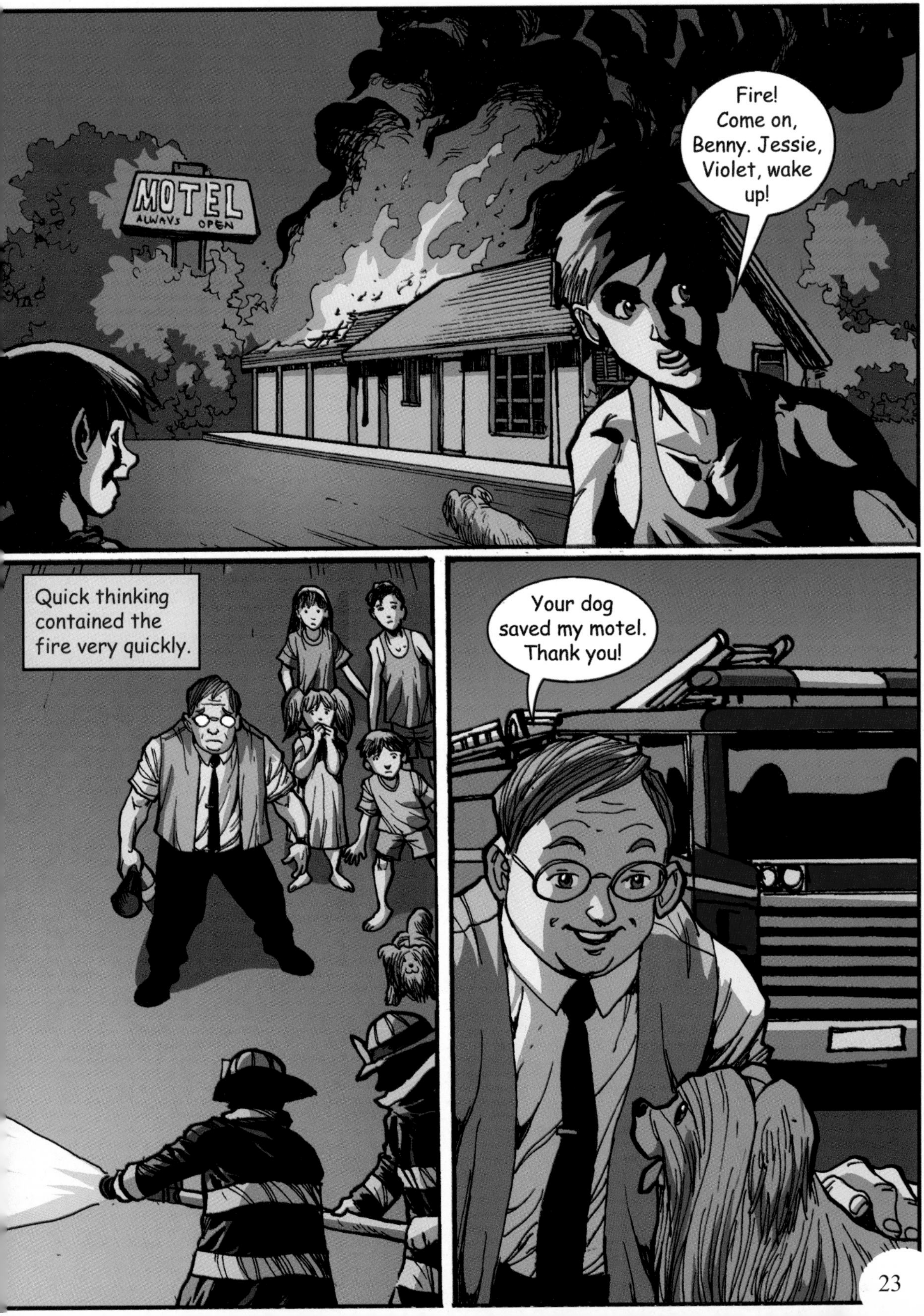
MOTEL
ALWAYS OPEN
Fire! Come on, Benny. Jessie, Violet, wake up!
Quick thinking contained the fire very quickly.
Your dog saved my motel. Thank you!

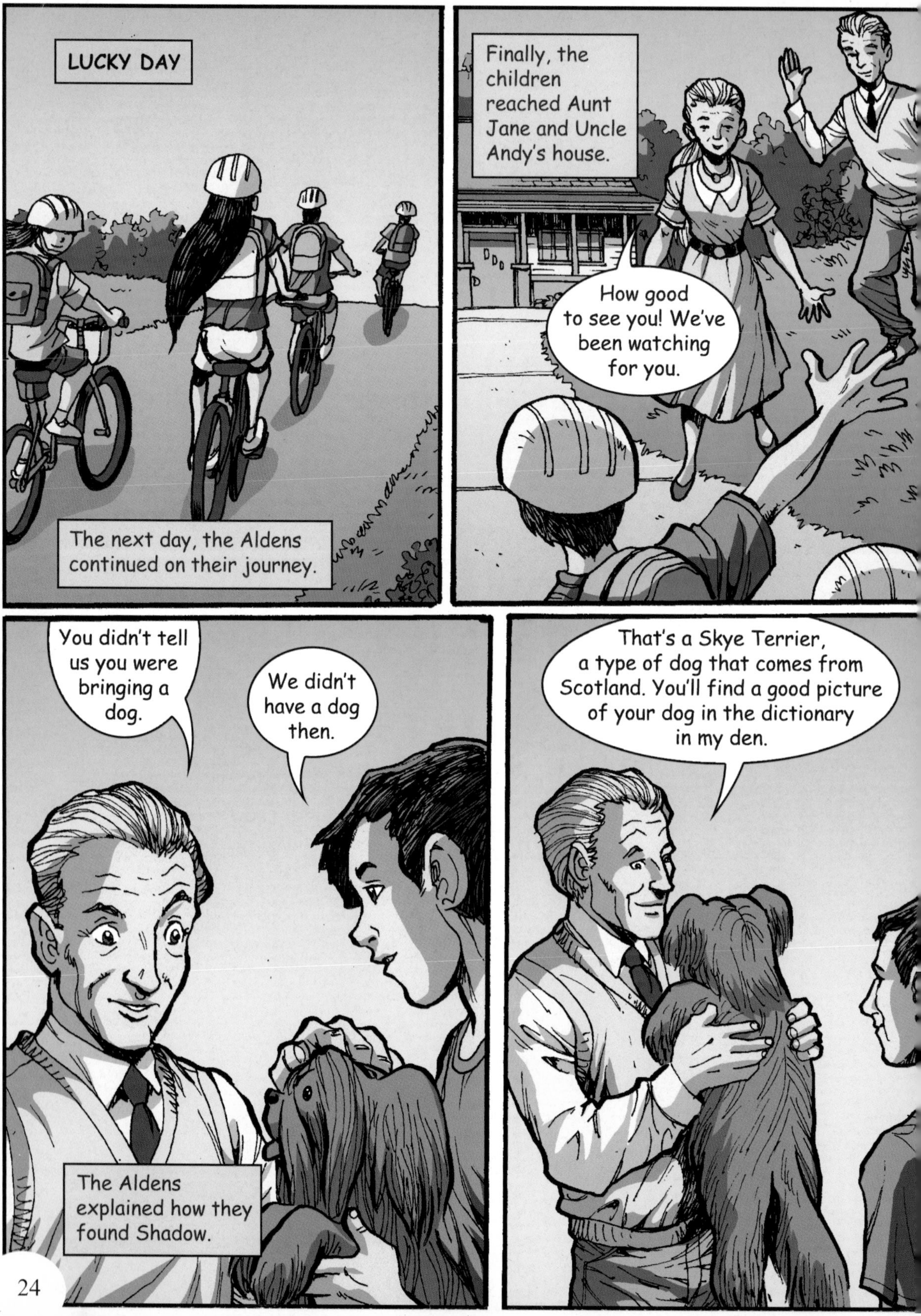
LUCKY DAY
The next day, the Aldens continued on their journey.
Finally, the children reached Aunt Jane and Uncle Andy's house.
How good to see you! We've been watching for you.
You didn't tell us you were bringing a dog.
We didn't have a dog then.
The Aldens explained how they found Shadow.
That's a Skye Terrier, a type of dog that comes from Scotland. You'll find a good picture of your dog in the dictionary in my den.

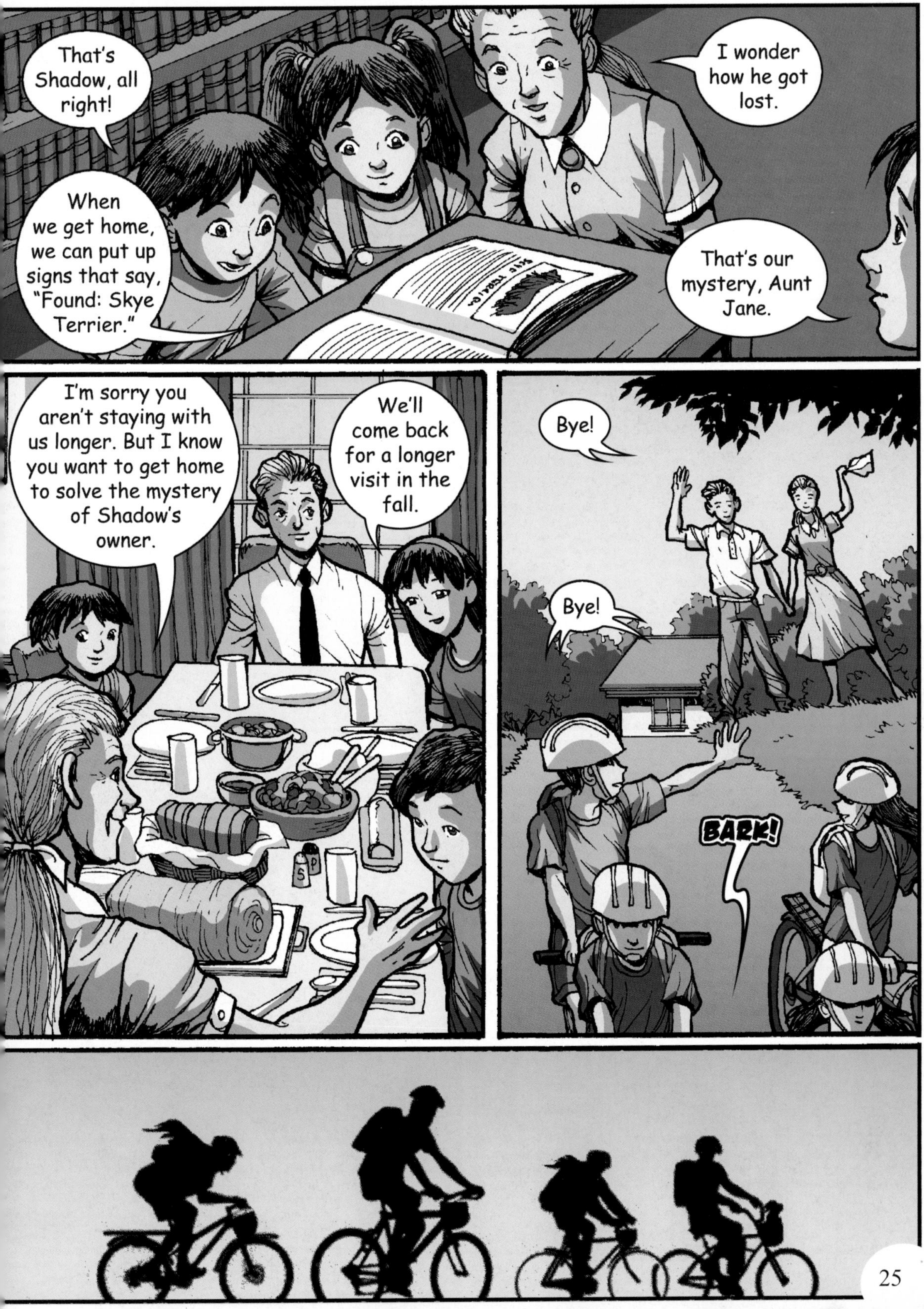
That's Shadow, all right!
When we get home, we can put up signs that say, "Found: Skye Terrier."
I wonder how he got lost.
That's our mystery, Aunt Jane.
I'm sorry you aren't staying with us longer. But I know you want to get home to solve the mystery of Shadow's owner.
We'll come back for a longer visit in the fall.
Bye!
Bye!
BARK!

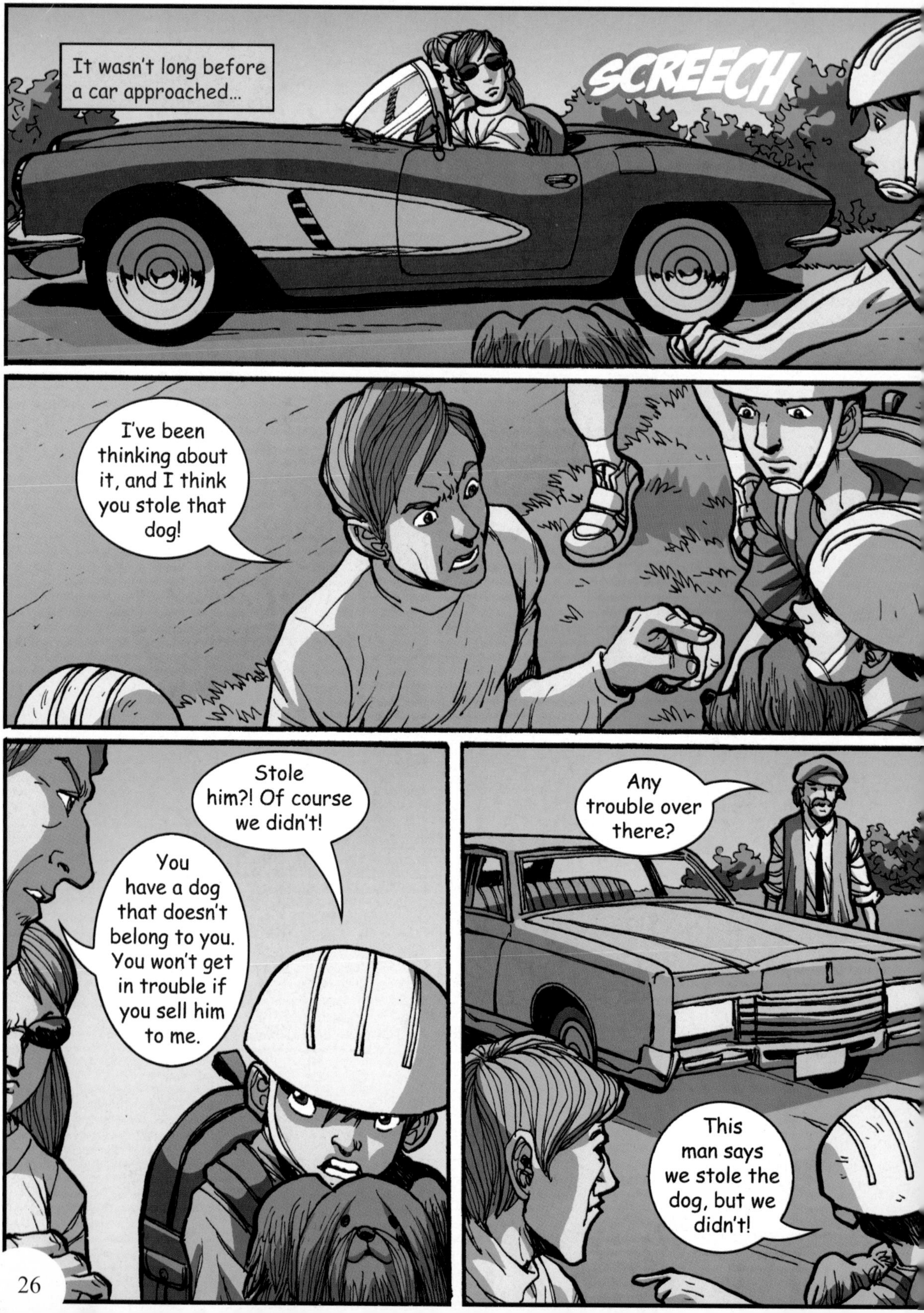
It wasn't long before a car approached...
SCREECH
I've been thinking about it, and I think you stole that dog!
Stole him?! Of course we didn't!
You have a dog that doesn't belong to you. You won't get in trouble if you sell him to me.
Any trouble over there?
This man says we stole the dog, but we didn't!

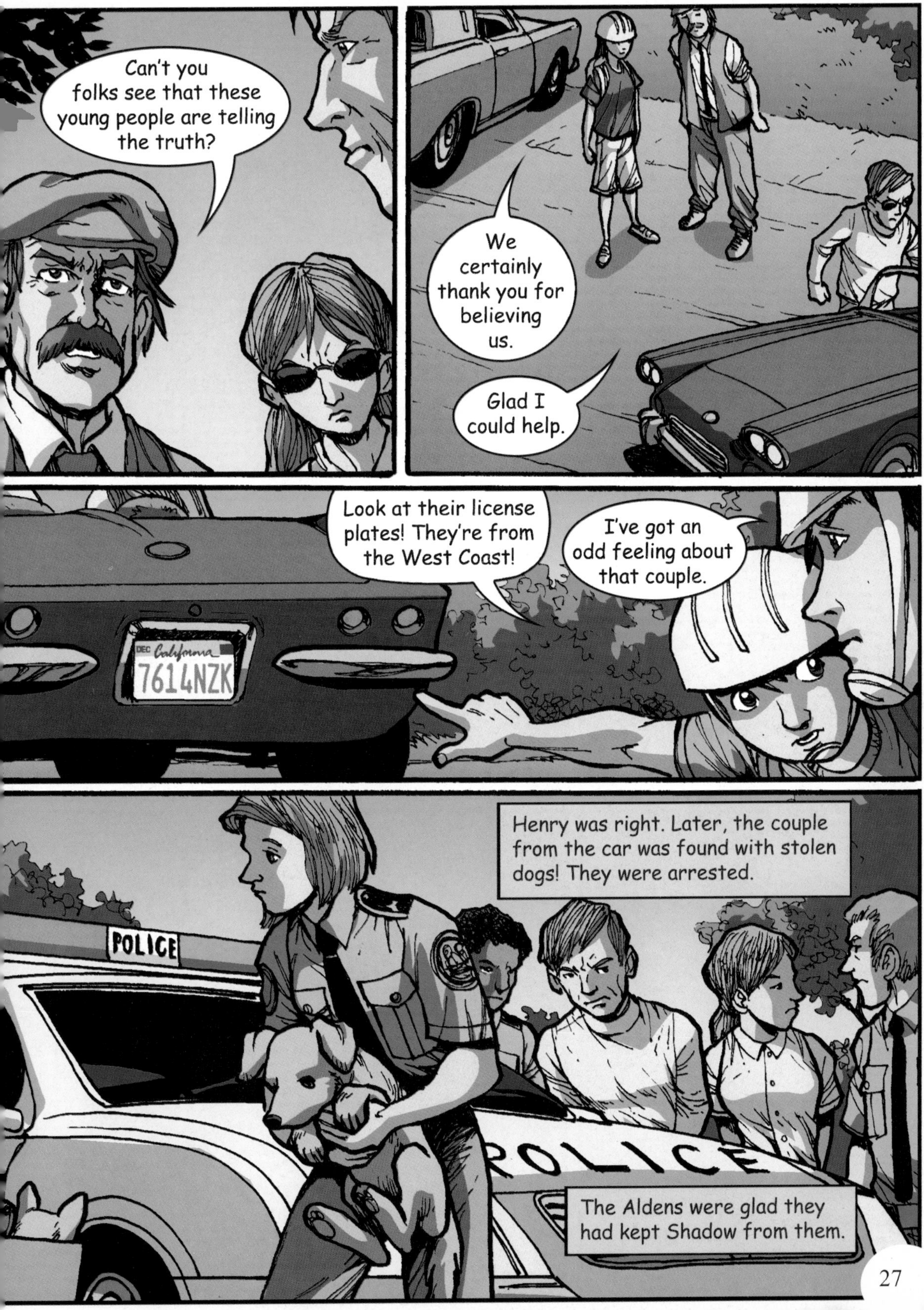
Can't you folks see that these young people are telling the truth?
We certainly thank you for believing us.
Glad I could help.
Look at their license plates! They're from the West Coast!
I've got an odd feeling about that couple.
DEC California
7614NZK
Henry was right. Later, the couple from the car was found with stolen dogs! They were arrested.
POLICE
POLICE
The Aldens were glad they had kept Shadow from them.

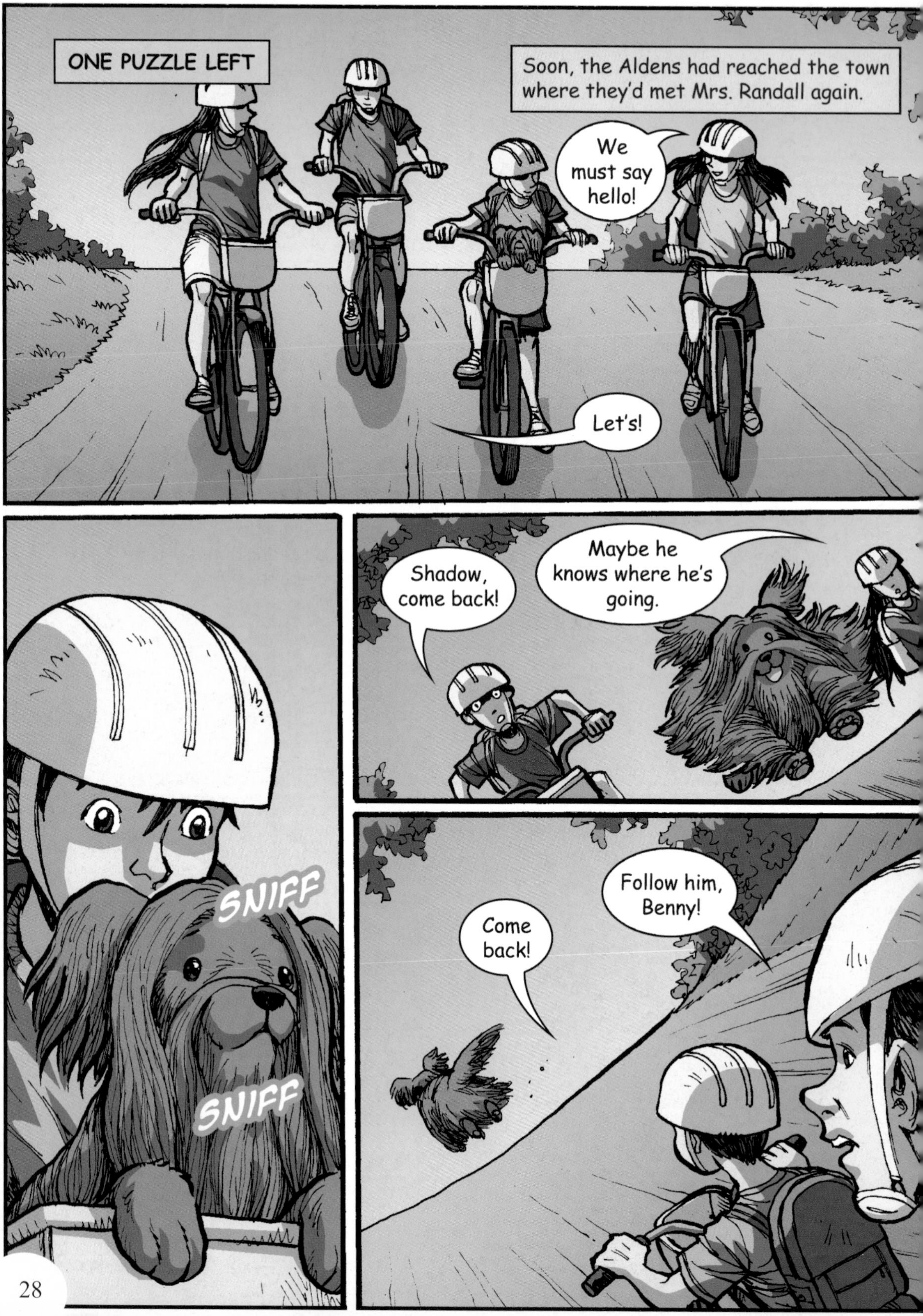
ONE PUZZLE LEFT
Soon, the Aldens had reached the town where they'd met Mrs. Randall again.
We must say hello!
Let's!
SNIFF
SNIFF
Shadow, come back!
Maybe he knows where he's going.
Come back!
Follow him, Benny!

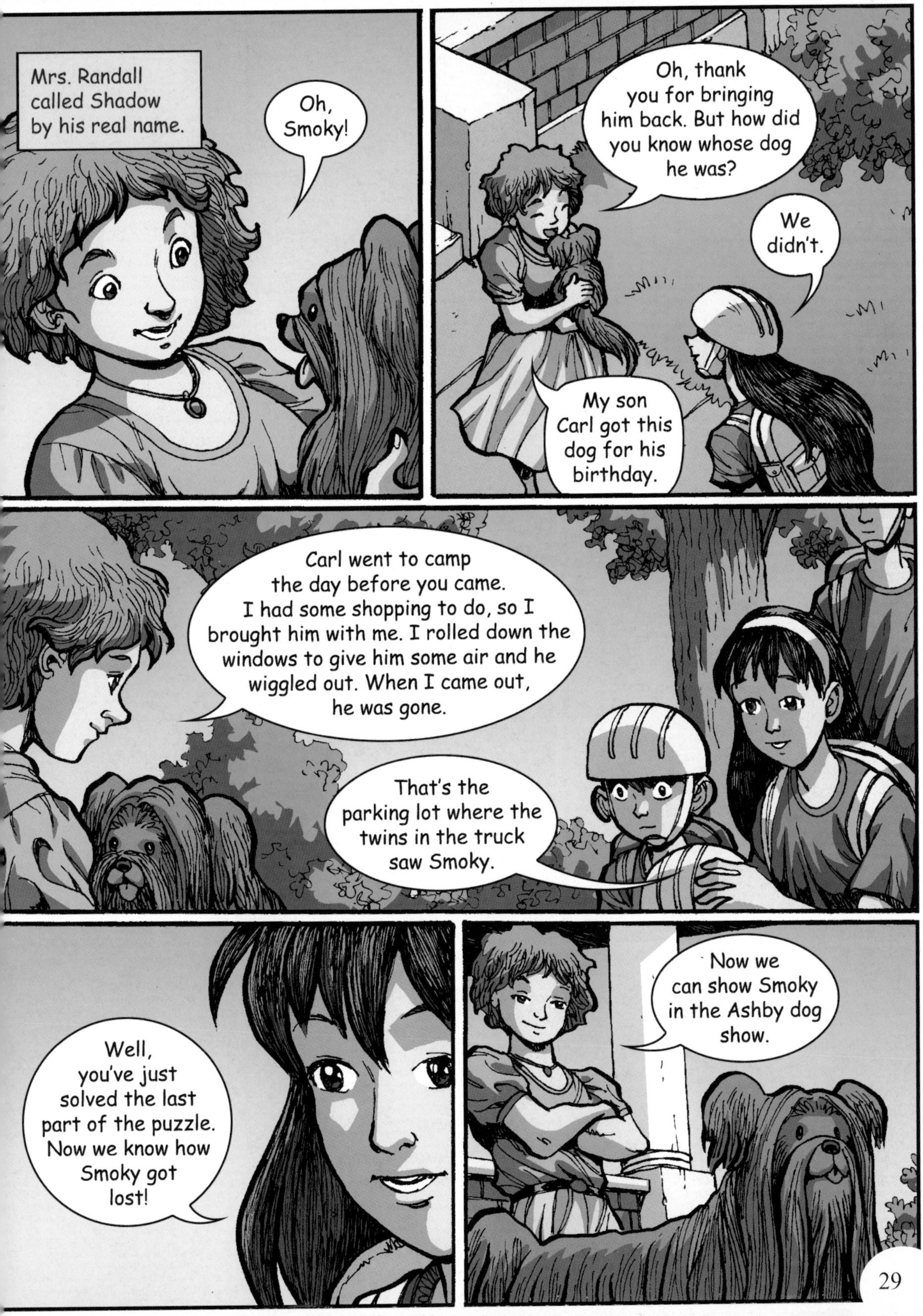
Mrs. Randall called Shadow by his real name.
Oh, Smoky!
Oh, thank you for bringing him back. But how did you know whose dog he was?
We didn't.
My son Carl got this dog for his birthday.
Carl went to camp the day before you came. I had some shopping to do, so I brought him with me. I rolled down the windows to give him some air and he wiggled out. When I came out, he was gone.
That's the parking lot where the twins in the truck saw Smoky.
Well, you've just solved the last part of the puzzle. Now we know how Smoky got lost!
Now we can show Smoky in the Ashby dog show.

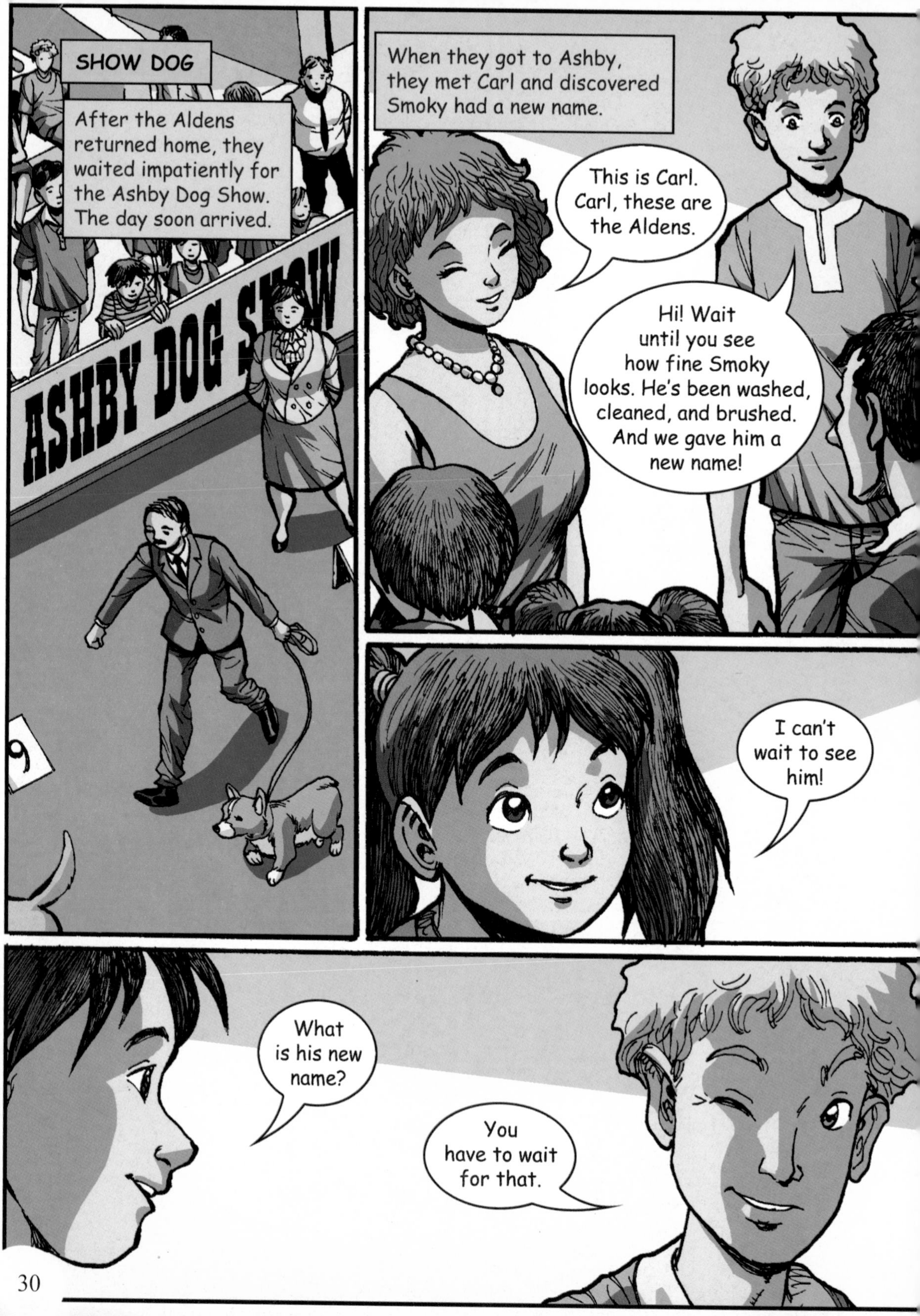
SHOW DOG
After the Aldens returned home, they waited impatiently for the Ashby Dog Show. The day soon arrived.
ASHBY DOG SHOW
When they got to Ashby, they met Carl and discovered Smoky had a new name.
This is Carl. Carl, these are the Aldens.
Hi! Wait until you see how fine Smoky looks. He's been washed, cleaned, and brushed. And we gave him a new name!
I can't wait to see him!
What is his new name?
You have to wait for that.

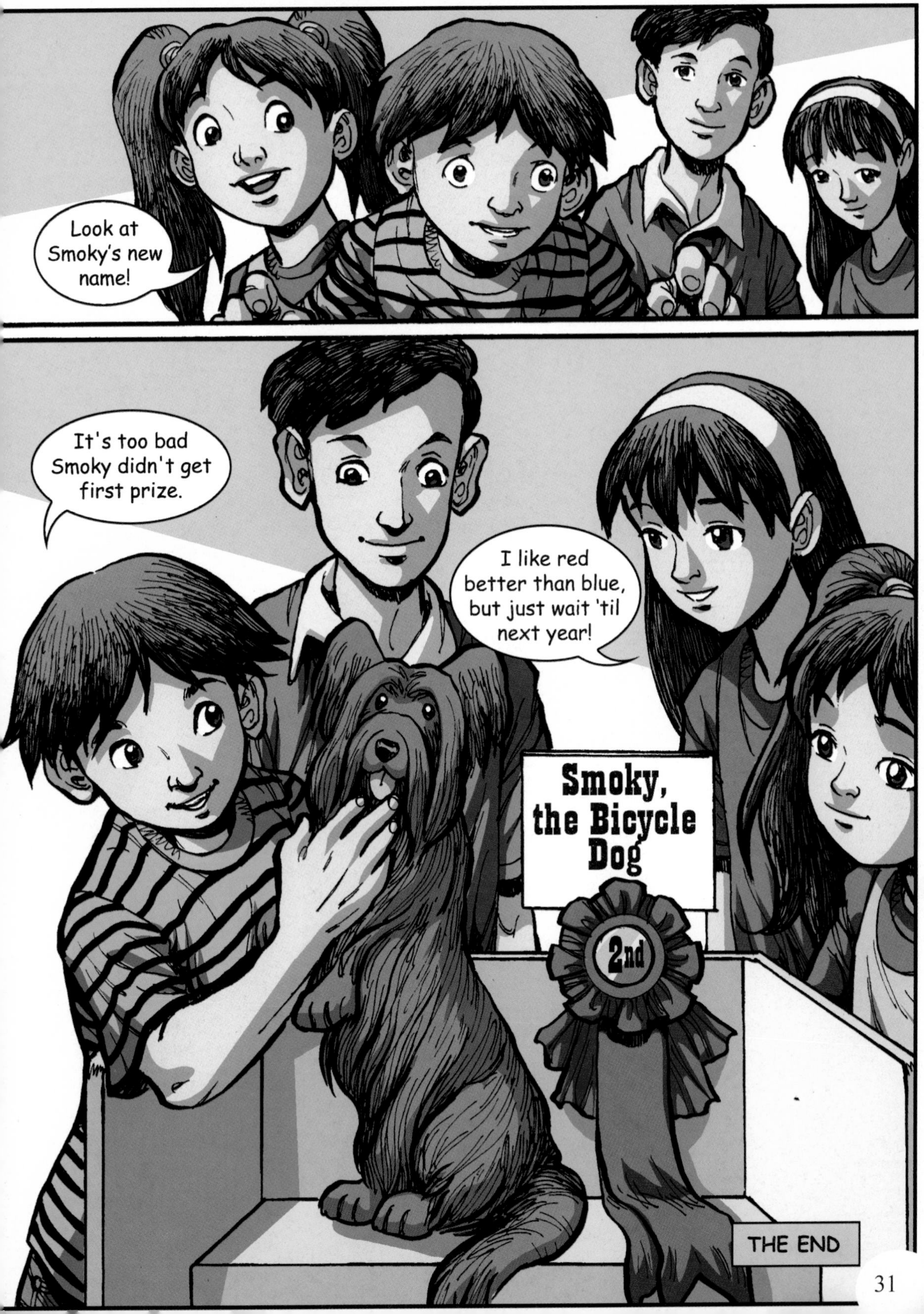
Look at Smoky's new name!
It's too bad Smoky didn't get first prize.
I like red better than blue, but just wait 'til next year!
Smoky, the Bicycle Dog
2nd
THE END

ABOUT THE CREATOR

Gertrude Chandler Warner was born on April 16, 1890, in Putnam, Connecticut. In 1918, Warner began teaching at Israel Putnam School. As a teacher, she discovered that many readers who liked an exciting story could not find books that were both easy and fun to read. She decided to try to meet this need. In 1942, *The Boxcar Children* was published for these readers.

Warner drew on her own experience to write *The Boxcar Children.* As a child she spent hours watching trains go by on the tracks near her family home. She often dreamed about what it would be like to live in a caboose or freight car—just as the Alden children do.

When readers asked for more Alden adventures, Warner began additional stories. While the mystery element is central to each of the books, she never thought of them as strictly juvenile mysteries. She liked to stress the Aldens' independence. Henry, Jessie, Violet, and Benny go about most of their adventures with as little adult supervision as possible—something that delights young readers.

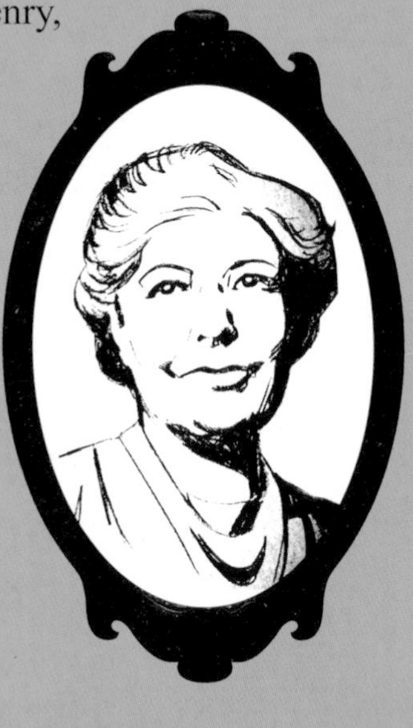

During her lifetime, Warner received hundreds of letters from fans as she continued the Aldens' adventures, writing nineteen Boxcar Children books in all. After her death in 1979, her publisher, Albert Whitman and Company, carried on Warner's vision. Today, the Boxcar Children series has more than 100 books.